ON THE HAPPY EDGE

On the Happy Edge
Third Edition – Published 2021
Published by Quality Rascal, L.L.C.
ISBN: 978-0-9992436-8-8

This book is based upon actual events and people. The author has tried to recreate events, locales and conversations from his memories of them. However, in order to maintain their anonymity and protect their privacy, the author has changed the names of individuals and places in which events took place throughout the book. He also changed the identifying characteristics and details such as physical properties, occupations and places of residence.

As such, these names, places, and characteristics are, in most cases, fictionalized. Any similarity between these fictitious names and descriptions to the name or attributes or actual background of any actual person, living or dead, or to any actual event, or to any existing company, is entirely coincidental, and unintentional. Notwithstanding the foregoing, some of the scenes in the book are inspired by real events – but have been fictionalized. The ending of the book is complete fiction.

Front and back book cover by Warren Red, L.L.C., New York, New York.
Photography by Mr. James Bareham of The New Cruelty, L.L.C., New York, New York.
To purchase additional copies, please see Amazon.com or e-mail info@qualityrascal.com.

TABLE OF CONTENTS

PREFACE

Sex, money, & murder." These words were tattooed on my "cousin's" underarm. When I was 18, I'd often ask myself: is that all life is about? One fateful night in Los Angeles 25 years ago, my answer to that question would change my life forever.

All of the people in the enclosed vignettes helped me understand my answer. This book is my way of saying thank you to them. The book is also an exploration of why strangers' objectivity is often the best salve for our demons within.

Of course, our fast-paced technologically infused world can give us a false sense of security. Silver bullet solutions are circulated. Short on money? Take an antidepressant. Having relationship issues? See a therapist. Shooting at your high school? Regulate guns. Want to find a good mate? Use artificial intelligence. We are led to believe that complex problems can be understood via a tweet, CNN sound bite, or Fox news alert. As a result, we never gain a holistic understanding of their causes. Our online world can, at times, eliminate the role of serendipity.

Complete strangers can help. As you will see, such understanding in the modern anarchy of life can be sitting next to you on the bus, train, or plane. Strangers that fate unexpectedly puts in our paths have the potential to provide more clarity than any modern peephole. They can often best illuminate one or more causes of your anxieties. Because they will never see you again, strangers don't sugar coat the truth or give you false hope. We have seen this advent of this phenomena in online communities where users remain anonymous. It also happens in open- source networks where complete strangers can constructively contribute to software.

To write this book, I culled numerous journal entries that I had been keeping for twelve years. The entries have helped me understand my decision as an 18 year old so many moons ago. I wrote the entries whenever I met someone who had an impact on me. In order to protect the privacy of the people featured herein, I changed their names, characteristics, professions and/or geographic locations, even my own. Except for the ending, the scenes in the book are based on real events – but have fictionalized.

Enjoy your read,
Ryan E. Long

PART I
ANGER

CHAPTER I

Street Fight

Loud and wasted, a handful of us had arrived at the house party in Venice Beach earlier in the evening. Reaching across a block with your index finger brought you to the Pacific Ocean's cold waters. Walking on water was but one of the things I thought I could do after drinking those two Crazy Horse 40 ounce bottles of malt liquor that night.

My name is Jack Egan. When I was 18, I thought stupor was my best friend. When I was 10, I thought math and Matthew Broderick, the nerdy hacker in "WarGames" (1983), were my best friends. In eight years, I had gone from shy nerd to furious teenager.

Fright and delight engulfed me inside the party. Scantily clad women, dope smoke, and the pounding sounds of "L.A. Woman" by The Doors surrounded me. I felt queasy so I stumbled outside with my friend Nicky Stravinska to smoke some Marlboro Reds. Beds, threads, and sneakers thrown on the sides of the street were our companions as we walked alongside the ocean's slow ebb and flow.

"Yo, man, take this one and finish it," I said to Nicky as I handed him my cigarette.

Several convertible Corvettes were parked along the street with their tops down. My dad had collected these cars. While at the time I frowned upon him and the cars, they still were not good candidates for my trickery. Luckily, I stumbled upon a convertible Rabbit VW. My memory was hazy, so I thought it was owned by this girl I knew. Wandering over to the car with alcohol-smelling sweat beading on my forehead, I poured some Crazy Horse beer into the driver's seat.

"Cool!" I thought as I did the deed.

Full of weed, intent on speed, and without need, I didn't notice the mob of black teenagers coming up the street. Feet surrounded Nicky and me as the leader yelled, "Hey, white boy." He pointed at me with his head cocked to the right. "Someone told me you just poured some shit into my girl's car."

As I looked at him, my eyebrows raised and the large scar on my forehead wrinkled.

"Dude, I am sorry," I said, shrugging. "I thought a girlfriend of mine owned that car."

"I don't give a fuck what you thought," the menacing leader said.

"Listen, I don't want any problems, dude. I'll clean it up. Just calm down, man." I put my palm out facing downwards and made a cooling motion.

"Don't tell me to calm down, white boy. Who the fuck do you think you are?" He pointed at my face with his long black index finger.

Lingering on his breath was an odor of salami and onion that had been left to rot in the park for days. Rays of anger from the black mob focused on me, the short, formerly nerdy, white boy from the San Fernando Valley. Tally and compute, I thought as I looked the leader up and down.

Frowning and down, with his jaw clinched tight, the boy stood about six feet in height. Wiry and dark, he was a stunt double for the rapper Snoop Dog. Flapper loose jeans and a long white t-shirt drooped on the boy's thin frame. As lame as I thought the jeans were, maybe they were hand-me-downs from an elder with squinty eyes and leathery skin, who lived close to his last breath.

Anger brewed in his eyes and in mine, too. We had more in common than I had originally thought. But his anger toward me was likely displaced. Of course, he still needed to rally in front of his friends. The real target of his rage was likely his family, his world, and/or himself.

"I fucked up, dude." I pushed my index finger into his chest. "But if you want to fight me, then let's scrap."

I pulled my finger off his chest.

Close to my breast was also a cancerous anger – toward my dead brother, toward my splintered family, and toward myself for not saving them all from the anarchy of life when I was I felt like burning myself to the ground for these failures, and anger was the best gasoline I could find. I was blind at the time to how much this anger had engulfed me. I am still learning, to this day, where it comes from and how to deal with it constructively.

But chess was the scrap that night, and my first move was to take off my white Jockey t- shirt in the

50-degree air. Frightened and shivering, my teeth chattered as I removed my t-shirt. The humid Venice evening air hit my skin. This was my first move.

"White boy is crazy" is what I wanted the black mob to think.

All of my trapped anger was now focused on the black boy's blinking eyes. Whether he was affected by it or not, I stared without blinking. Featherweight-like, his white t-shirt showed his toned muscles as he gave his jacket to one of his friends.

Ducking under his big right swing at me was my second move, followed by my third, tackling the prick to the sandpaper concrete below.

Bam! Both of us crashed to the ground after I slammed him.

After I quickly maneuvered to his backside, I wrapped my right leg around his body and pushed my right heel onto his privates. As I did, I pressed my right knee into his abdomen. His long powerful body was now pinned on the ground.

As I smashed his balls with my foot, I squeezed his Adam's apple. He started gasping for his life as we lay by the tire of a parked car.

From far away, kicks from one of his friends swiftly hit my back. Bam, bam, bam, bam! The boy's kicks whaled on my ribs.

Numb to pain, I choked him harder.

His crew in Starter® Raiders jackets then surrounded me and started battering my body with a chorus of their kicks. Kick, kick, kick . . . . kick, kick, kick . . . kick, kick, kick, the feet slammed onto my body like organized pistons in some fine tuned machine.

I let go of the boy, covered my head, and crumpled into a fetal position for what seemed like a year. Suddenly, the kicking stopped. I was afraid that one of the boys had taken out a pistol. To my relief, that wasn't why the kicking had stopped. Instead, a cavalry of my friends had run out from the party to throw bombs of fists and body slams on the boys.

Dylan Egan was a six-foot-four Irish cousin of mine from the football team. According to family lore, one of our family members, Mickey, was an Irish Don from Boston and American spy who fought in French Resistance during World War II. He used his redwood-sized arms and legs to pile-drive one of the boy's heads into the ground while holding his ankles. As I lay on the ground, drenched in blood and covered in scratches, I wondered to myself: how in the world did Dylan get him in a WWF wrestling hold?

Everyone ran to their cars after one of the neighbors yelled, "We're calling the cops!" But the cops never came.

Dylan, Nicky, and the others helped me get up off the ground. That's when I went inside to take a shower.

I didn't know the blood on my body was my own until I was in the shower. As the blood washed away, a constellation of deep, screwdriver-sized stab wounds appeared on my right shoulder and ribcage. Because I had been so drunk earlier that night, I hadn't even felt the tips of the screwdrivers park themselves in the driveway of my skin.

At the time, I was proud about not feeling them. Now, I am ashamed.

When I got out of the shower, I put some gauze over the wounds, wrapped a towel around my waist, and called "Frank White," real name Jesse Hardin.

"Frank, it's Saturn."

Frank used to affectionately call me "Saturn" because I drove a Saturn SL1, the first of its kind made in Tennessee, the land of Andrew Jackson.

"What's up, Saturn," Frank answered.

Frank was not a nice-looking person, but he was a nice person to me. He sported a long hillbilly goatee and kept his head shaven. He had massive Popeye forearms and large biceps, coupled with Neanderthal hands. Tattoos were plastered all over his arms; he was sleeved up with tricked-out hot rods, motorcycles, jokers, and strippers. I didn't know what the Japanese tattoo under his right armpit meant until we took a trip to New Mexico. As we drove along with the orange-colored mountain range in the background, I asked Frank. He sat calmly in the passenger seat with his lean jujitsu body and told me: "Sex, money, and murder, Saturn."

"Dude, I just got jumped at a party," I told Frank over the phone that night in Venice. "I think one of them stabbed me with a screwdriver!" I remember shivering with fear, anger, and guilt for having gotten my friends into the mess.

"Where are you?" Frank asked calmly. "Venice." I gave him the address.

"I'll be there in about half an hour. Can you make it until then?" he asked.

"Yeah. I think I can. I should be able to." It looked like the bleeding had slowed down. "Good. Meet me outside."

It felt as if I were outside for less than a minute when Frank's 1984 Chevrolet Monte Carlo SS screamed around the corner. I could hear its horsepower from a block away. It was a nice muscle car made by Chevy and had a NASCAR look to it. Frank's SS was Darth Vader black with custom silver rims, tinted black windows, and a tricked-out engine.

When the car stopped, the passenger door creaked opened like a casket top in a Halloween movie. I got into the back seat. The Allman Brothers' song, "Midnight Rider," was playing loudly. Frank wrapped me in a Mexican beach blanket and closed the car door.

Paula, Frank's "old lady," was driving. She was a rough but pretty sleeved-up brunette with taut gymnast muscles. I had seen her knock out a girl who was trying to light the long Anthony Kiedis hair of Butch Amos, one of Frank's associates who looked like a 1980s Wild West looking *Playgirl* model, in a Venice bar.

Another associate of Frank's, a guy named Vick, was in the back seat. He was a tattooed Valley boy who did a lot of business with various gangs in Los Angeles.

Frank and Mick had UZI submachine guns resting softly on their laps like pet cats. I also knew that Frank had his Heckler & Koch ("HK") .9 mm pistol under his seat. He always kept an HK under the passenger seat of his cars and trucks.

As we tore off toward the freeway, Frank coolly turned down the "Midnight Rider" song. It played softly in the background like make-out music. Rustic-looking, like the gun-slinging cowboy who wears a black hat, Frank slowly turned around, glaring at me with his corn blue eyes for a few seconds, and then softly asked, "Saturn, where are they?"

I didn't know it then, but my answer to Frank's question would affect the rest of my life. I didn't understand the source of my cancerous anger that night until I turned 29 and started seeing a psychiatrist in New Orleans. By then, I was hopeless, drinking, and smoking dope every day.

CHAPTER 2

Frank White Loves Me

"So who is this Frank White?" Dr. Shun Ling Wu, the New Orleans psychiatrist who I affectionately called "Dr. Ling," asked me.

I thought to myself, well, Dr. Ling, he is a murdering psychopath who is like my surrogate older brother. But I didn't want to be a smart alek, so I answered the best I could.

"Frank is a friend of mine who I met when I was 16." His name is Jesse Hardin, but nobody every used his real name, always calling him Frank White. I was no exception. I shrugged as if Frank were a high school teacher. "I met him at the gym . . . but . . . whatever." I pictured bleachers full of fans cheering at my ducking of the question.

"No," Dr. Ling insisted, "tell me. Don't give me the 'whatever.' That's a cop out, like your dad's cop out."

Body blows can knock people out, and his was a good one. And while brawn is nice to have, a sharp mind, like Dr. Ling's, is more effective. I contemplated this as I paused in the middle of his office to look around. Old bound books and photos of family and friends covered his living room walls, in addition to a small menagerie: a boar's head, a fowl in a glass, and a black onyx skull. Out the window I could see Spanish colonial arches shrouded by the trees lining the quaint Governor Nichols Street in the middle of the French Quarter.

Aging and graying, Dr. Ling, the Chinese sage from Hong Kong, was about 80 at the time. His pretty Danish wife prayed every Sunday, but she accidentally interrupted our sessions one or two times by barging into the living room wearing lingerie.

Dr. Ling was full of knowledge but slight in size at about five-foot-five. While he didn't know jive, he had a pretty soul nonetheless. He usually dressed in simpleton jeans, ate beans, and knew the means of getting through life with a bad gait, a hearing aid, and a dead son. Fun and decrepit like much of New Orleans, Dr. Ling and his office were familiar and cozy. But he was not lazy: he published numerous articles in publications and did laps naked in the backyard pool every day.

I remember the day I found him. I woke up one morning, prepared a proper joint, brewed some coffee, and went to sit by the pool. While I sipped my coffee and got high with Alby, a friend of mine who you'll meet shortly, I scoured the phone book for psychiatrists. I found Dr. Ling's name and called him. When I heard his raspy voice over the phone, my intuition told me he would be a good fit.

My intuition turned out to be right.

Day and night I would smoke, booze, and fret whenever I was not at one of my monthly sessions with the dilapidated looking but lovely doctor. I saw him over a two-year period while I was living in New Orleans. The following segment is a condensed version of several sessions I had with him. The same is true of the other sessions sprinkled throughout the book. All of these sessions were the most memorable to me. Trouble had bubbled, and I was there to better understand my feelings of anger and its cousin, fear. I redoubled my efforts to open up:

"When I first met Frank, he asked me for a spot."

"What's a spot?" Dr. Ling asked.

"When you help someone lift weights . . . you make sure the weights don't slam down on him when he is tired from lifting."

"Alright, so he asks for a spot, and?" Dr. Ling nodded so as to encourage me to proceed. "I give him one. He was bench pressing 225 pounds like a feather." I briefly looked up at Dr. Ling's ornate ceiling to remember my first meeting with Frank in the smelly, sweaty, macho gym. I then continued, "He did like three sets at 15 reps each." I made a pressing motion away from my chest with both hands like I was lifting the weight right in front of Dr. Ling.

"So he is physically strong. How old is he?"

"Ten years older than me . . . I think my sister's age. So he is about 39 . . . I actually introduced Frank to my sister's husband, soon to be ex-husband, and they became friends."

"So Frank was a mentor to you, in a way?"

"Yes," I nodded. "He took me under his wing."

"What does he do for a living? I mean, is he a professional? A doctor?" Ling asked. "A damn good professional," I paused, "and he is sort of a doctor."

"Meaning?" Ling asked.

Leaning closer to him in my chair, I laid it on him. "Let me give you the character profile, and I'm sure you figure out what he is about."

"Alright," Ling adjusted himself in his seat, crossed his legs, and took a sip of his organic mint tea.

"Frank drove nice cars. Real nice cars: a pitch black 1984 Chevrolet Monte Carlo SS, a black 1988 Ferrari Testarossa, a black souped-up Chevy 454 SS Truck." I was hinting to Dr. Ling like a coy lover who does not want to reveal his true feelings of love. "And a number of motorcycles: Ducatis, Buells, Nortons, and Triumphs."

Potholes were strewn all over the street outside, so the booze-filled truck, heading to lose itself in the stomach of some boozers in the bowels of the quarter, cracked and smacked as it passed by the windows of Dr. Ling's Shangri-la.

"So Frank liked motorcycles and cars?" Dr. Ling took a loud sip of his tea like the old man next to you at lunch that annoys you with his old-man sounds.

"Pounds and pounds of them. And you knew never to expect him before noon."

"Why?" Ling asked.

"Because he never woke up until noon. He usually went to sleep around two or three in the morning. That is when most of his business was done, so noon was the start of his work day."

"Day is night, night is day?" Dr. Ling took another sip of his tea. "That sounds odd."

"Add to that the HK 9mm pistol always hidden under the passenger seat of any car he drove. He'd roam around the streets of Los Angeles with the small arsenal he did not show, but people in his business knew he had."

"He had other weapons?" Dr. Ling asked with an eyebrow raised.

"At home he had others: an UZI submachine gun in his bedroom dresser, an HK 9 millimeter pistol under his pillow, rifles and machine guns in the vault in the pool room."

"Vroom!" Dr. Ling exclaimed with a playful smirk. "Just like that he leaves the house never without his American Express?"

"Impressed?" I looked at Dr. Ling intently.

"Dressed, or not, in color, I can get the picture here, Jack. But weren't you concerned with all of those guns being around?"

"I won't give you roundabout answers, Dr. Ling. I loved Frank, plain and simple. Pimples all over my face and without a feeling of grace, I proudly called him 'cousin,' and he did the same to me," I said, thinking back. "I didn't mind the arsenal, as long as it came with my cousin behind it."

"Why?" Dr. Ling asked.

"He cared about me," I said with another shrug, "and I cared about him, but you wouldn't understand."

Trim and simple, Dr. Ling probably sat in his seat wandering the depths of my mind and wondering how I could befriend such a monster.

"Try me," he said. "How did he love you?"

His willingness to kill for me was not something I wanted to mention to Dr. Ling. Bring something else to him, I thought to myself. "He took care of me after I moved back to Los Angeles, before I moved here to New Orleans."

"And you came back here after traveling overseas for some time after 9/11? I think you mentioned that to me over the phone."

"Traveling alone," I nodded.

"You worked at the large law firm in New York before that?"

"Feeling alone."

"How did he take care of you?" Dr. Ling took another sip of his tea.

"I stayed with him in Venice Beach when I got back from my travels. He gave me an extra room in his house. We would split the groceries and have dinner together. He was always making sure that I was being proactive in my life–whether it was working, doing chores around the house, or dating."

I looked out Dr. Ling's apartment window toward the bright New Orleans sun shining and then turned back to him:

"I remember he would always tell me, 'Do as I say, not as I do.'"

"And what did he mean when he said 'Do as I say, not as I do'?"

"He wanted me to make something of myself. He used to tell me, 'Get out of L.A. and create a life of your own, Saturn.'" He used to tell me, 'Get out of here, go to school, make money, enjoy your life' Whether I knew it or not at the time, that night and

Frank, were instrumental in causing me to move to Chicago, which is where I transferred to go to college."

Dr. Ling paused to look up at his bookshelf, and then looked back at me. "But you obviously formed a bond with him before the night you are mentioning. How?"

"Well, during the summers we would often go to the beach with Paula."

"And Paula was his girlfriend?"

"Right."

"Got it." Dr. Ling drank some of his herbal tea. "What was Paula like?"

"She was a feminine but toned woman about five foot six, with brown hair and hazelnut eyes. We used to go with her to the beach during the summer in Frank's Chevrolet El Camino."

"Just you three?"

"No. He would always hook me up with girls he knew. 'Get in the back with the girls, Saturn. I think you'll like them,' he used to tell me in his gruff voice. 'Yea, Saturn, get in the back with us,' the two or three young women would say to me, in their Daisy Duke jean shorts, tank tops and slip on Vans. They usually sported unruly hair and covered up their toned bodies with small surfer-girl bikinis."

"What did you guys do at the beach?"

"Frank and I would take walks and talk about our families with the waves of the Pacific in the background."

"What did he say? What did he say about your family?"

"He used to tell me, 'It's not your fault, Saturn, that your dad has given up. It's his decision. Not yours. You can only do so much to help him. At some point, you can only live your life and do the best with it that you can.'"

"Solid advice," Dr. Ling said with a surprised tone and a raised eyebrow. "Totally. And when Paula and Frank broke up, he impressed me."

"How?"

"Well, he told me, 'Paula is my girl and I'll always be her friend, Saturn.'"

"Did he live up to that?" Ling asked.

I readjusted myself in Dr. Ling's comfy worn brown leather couch. "I think so. At one point Paula started going out with a trashy boyfriend who would hurt her. He was some type of 'Peckerwood,' which is a white supremacist gang. Paula would often call Frank and confide in him. I overheard their conversations, and remember Frank's tenor. 'Paula, you deserve better than this pig is giving you. Why don't you leave him?'"

"So it seems Frank had great advise for others in terms of dating, work, and life, in general. . . but did he follow his own sage advice?"

"Well, that is why he used to tell me to do what he said, not what he did. I formed the impression he was on a path toward self-destruction."

"Why?"

CHAPTER 3

Boys Don't Cry

"Frank was angry at his father for leaving when he was younger. But Frank secretly blamed himself. It's like he thought he did something wrong to cause his father to abandon them," I said in an uncertain tone.

"And what did the anger do to him?" Dr. Ling asked.

"I think it kept him alive. It kept him going. Without the anger, I don't know that he would still be around."

"So you believe in anger?" Dr. Ling asked.

"It has its place. When you are in danger, you get angry. It serves a biological purpose."

"I understand that at times you need to protect yourself and that anger can be a sign that something is wrong. But, generally, I have seen anger as a way for people, especially men, to avoid having emotions. It's like the only way for you to express your emotions is by being angry," Dr. Ling pointed out.

"As opposed to being horribly sad?" I asked.

"Precisely," he nodded. "Sadness is weakness for many men. If you are sad, you are weak, as they say. If you are mad, then you are powerful," he pounded his right fist on his chest, "a force to be reckon with. Someone –"

"Not to be fucked with," I interrupted.

"Right. Not to be fucked with," Dr. Ling finished. "Do you know the group The Cure?" I asked. "No. Who's that?"

"It's an English music group."

"Alright. What about them?"

"They have a song called 'Boys Don't Cry.'"

"And that is what you learned growing up?" I looked at him with a short stare.

"Yes."

"And who taught you that?"

"My father."

"Why do you think he taught you that?"

"If you cried as a man, you were weak. That is the law of jungle, is it not? I mean, if you are in the playground, on the street, in the boardroom and you cry, you are perceived as a weak man."

"But are you weak, Jack, if you cry?"

I paused. I was uncertain of how to answer at the time.

Dr. Ling moved his legs and crossed them the other way as he got into the conversation, kind of like a boxer who has warmed up after the first round and is now hitting his stride. He continued with his effective jabs.

"Do you think that your father was strong by not crying?" I came back from being on the ropes and jabbed back.

"I don't think it matters whether you are, in fact, weak if you cry. Perception is everything. If you cry, and you are a man, you are *perceived to be* weak, even by women who complain about the types of brutal Alpha men featured in movies like "Mean Streets" or in shows like "Mad Men," I didn't make the rules. They were there for me to follow, Dr. Ling." I looked back at him as though I got around his jab and came back with a body punch. Dr. Ling continued, nonetheless, with his pressing questions:

"But didn't that anger trap Frank into one identity: an astute and wicked gangster?"

"He is still living, right?" I quickly responded. "I mean, he's never been in the can. He lives a life of relative leisure. While other schmucks bust their humps working nine-to-five jobs for people that don't care about them, Frank wakes up late in the day. He has control over his life and does as he pleases."

I gave Dr. Ling a self-satisfied smile.

"There is a cost to that." He looked at me with concern. "Freedom isn't free," I retorted.

"This is something we need to talk about more."

"What?"

"Your worship of anger," he said in a grave tone. "In my professional opinion, and I'm telling this to you as your psychiatrist, uncontrolled anger only leads to more anger, against yourself and against others. It is cancerous."

He paused to let it sink in.

"Real courage is persistently facing your problems and confronting them with love, compassion, and understanding," he continued.

At the time, his comment went right over my head. I started learning the wisdom of his comments later on in my life, but I was clueless at the time so I retorted with another punch.

"That sounds nice, Dr. Ling, but do you think that the world operates that way? It doesn't. People *don't* confront their problems with love, compassion, and understanding."

"What you say reminds me of the character from Truman Capote's *In Cold Blood* . . . the boy who killed the family in Kansas. Do you remember?"

"I think his name was James. James. . . James something."

"Latham."

"Right, that's him. Latham," I nodded in agreement.

"Latham said something like, 'it's a rotten world. There's no answer to it but meanness. That's all that anybody understands–meanness. Burn down the man's barn, he'll understand that. Poison his dog. Kill him.' Do you remember that?"

"I seem to," I said.

"And what do you think?"

"I think he was generally right," I said. "People usually don't understand kindness and compassion. Like he said, ruthless brutality is all people seem to really pay attention to these days. If you are nice to people, they take advantage of you. They seem to see it as a sign of weakness. I mean, haven't you ever heard the phrase, 'nice guys finish last'?" I asked.

"Yes," Dr. Ling nodded.

"Where do you think that comes from? It was there when I was born, and it will be there when I die. I actually think there is a book out there now called something like '*Only Assholes Win*.'"

"So what?"

"So what? If I'm just some jaded asshole who is an outlier, then why is there all this literature out there that is so popular our culture?"

"And don't you think that these assholes, as you call them, eventually, one way or another, get theirs?" Dr. Ling asked.

"Like karma?" I asked.

"Yes, like karma," Ling emphasized.

"I just don't know. I have seen so many non-karma oriented people who make it to the top, like in Los Angeles. Agents, lawyers, or managers–you name it," I said in a frustrated tone, like he wasn't hearing me.

"But if you look into the personal lives of many of these people," Dr. Ling retorted, "you will see, in many but not all cases that they are a mess: divorces, mistresses, unhappy children. A lot of these people are afraid to look at themselves in the mirror, to see that they are fallible humans and not gods. This is, in large part, why the world is in such a mess – ego run amok," he looked out the window and then looked back at me.

"Perhaps the world would be in more of a mess and there would be more chaos if there wasn't that power structure?" I said. "Great white sharks exist for a reason."

"Listen, we'll continue this discussion later. I understand your outlook. Many people have it. At the same time, I think it is going to lead you into otherwise avoidable problems. If it hasn't already led you to them, it has with others."

"We all have problems; I just have my own set of them, Dr. Ling," I said contemptuously.

Perhaps he is right I asked myself? I wondered when I sat there in Dr. Ling's office whether there was another way. Maybe I had been taught about anger and holding in my emotions all my life without ever having explored other answers. Dr. Ling interrupted my thoughts with his next question.

"Isn't that why you are here? To talk about your depression, your outbursts of anger, and your everyday pot smoking? These are rhetorical questions, Jack," he said smiling. "So let me ask you. What do you think caused this anger originally for you?"

"I don't know." I shrugged.

"Let me ask you this. Have you ever lost anybody in your family?"

"Yes."

"Who?"

"My brother."

"And what was his name?"

"Liam."

"What happened?" Dr. Ling poured some more hot tea into his cup. "Why does it matter?" I asked, sort of annoyed.

"Well, maybe you have some of the same reasons to be angry that Frank has, but never really took heed of them in your life. Your anger has numbed you."

When he said that, I thought back to the night in Venice Beach. I thought about how both the booze and the anger that I had inside me had caused the chaos of the evening but also numbed me from the stabbing. I then let Dr. Ling know about Liam.

"The right side of my brother's skull was shattered into pieces when he was 16. The VW thing that he was riding slid uncontrollably into a flatbed truck parked in the emergency lane of the rain-slicked 101 freeway in Los Angeles."

"Why do you focus on the head?" Dr. Ling asked as he took another sip of his tea. I paused to think about his question for a moment.

"Because at the funeral he had artificial hair put there to cover up the gaping wound that the truck had left." I pointed my index finger to the back of my head where my brother's wound had been. "The image of that light spot in the middle of his dark brown head has impregnated my mind."

"How old were you at the time?"

"I was 10."

"How do you know what happened to him?"

"Everybody in the car survived except Liam. All of them told the police that the driver bent over to pick up a tape that had fallen near the gas pedal. Then the car slid into the flat bed truck."

"Do you think you have come to peace with his death?" Ling asked. "In some ways, yes, but in some ways, no," I said.

"What are you, a politician?" Dr. Ling asked. "I feel like you're a politician on the campaign trail who answers a question from a reporter that you really don't want to answer." Dr. Ling leaned forward like an eager reporter to hear my response. "Sir, did you sleep with that woman?" He paused. "In some ways, yes, but in some ways, no," he said with a wide grin.

I shot him a grateful smile.

"So, how have you been in denial?"

"I never cried about my brother dying."

"Not even once in your life?" Dr. Ling asked.

"Not once," I said with emphasis.

"Boy's don't cry, right?" He looked at me sympathetically. I stared back coldly and defiantly.

Frank would have been proud, I thought to myself.

"Well, why do you think you got into that fight in Venice, Jack?" I shrugged my shoulders.

"Your anger," he said, as if he knew something I didn't.

It was fine that he knew and I didn't. That's why I thought I had gone to see him.

I looked out the window in Dr. Ling's living room to reflect on what he had said, but I was so tethered to the idea of Frank's way of life as I sat there that my mind was short-circuited, preventing me from seeing other possibilities.

Dr. Ling waited patiently for me, and then he pushed things along. "But that was really just sadness pent up inside you, wasn't it, Jack? Just as the man whom you fought had sadness pent up inside him."

"Like two jack–in-the-boxes fighting one another?" I jested. "If you want to put it that way, then yes."

I paused to look at him.

"And so that fight was an attempt to let it out?" I asked with piqued interest. I wondered if he had a point.

"You got it," he said.

"Have you ever cried?" I asked him. "Yes, of course. Crying is healthy, Jack."

"When did you cry?"

"One time was when my son got married," Ling answered. "I was so happy for him to have found the woman he did. And you, Jack, have you ever cried?"

I thought for a moment.

"The first time was when I was 26. My girlfriend Juliette and I had moved to New York, but two weeks after we got to the city, she left and moved back to France."

"Damn French!" Dr. Ling exclaimed. "They give up, just like in WWII!" I smirked at him. I started to like him more throughout the session. "You must have been very angry at her."

"I was. I remember lying in bed at night crying. I didn't sleep much. I would go to work and couldn't function properly. I fell into a deep depression. That is when I started smoking grass heavily and taking antidepressants. I thought moving back here, to New Orleans, would make things better."

"But?" Dr. Ling asked. "But it didn't," I answered.

"And that is why you came to see me? To get help?" I nodded. He paused for a moment.

"Well, let me ask you this. Do you think your depression came only from her?" Dr. Ling asked, staring into my eyes.

I knew he was trying to get at something. "I suppose so."

"But you never cried about your brother and family. You kept it all inside for sixteen years?"

"Right," I nodded.

"So, perhaps when she left, it triggered all of those feelings you had when you were younger, but never allowed yourself to feel."

"I guess so."

"Do you think anything about your experience at that large law firm you told me about over the phone had an effect on you, too?" He watched me while he sipped his tea.

I shrugged.

"Maybe. In law school we were given this impression of what that life would be like in a large law firm. It seemed so enchanting. And yet when I got there, it wasn't what I thought it would be like."

"Which is?"

"Fulfilling."

"And it wasn't?"

"It wasn't. I felt empty for some reason."

"You were in denial all of those years, Jack. It seems you had an image of what you wanted your family to be like, and it wasn't like that. You thought Juliette was one way, but she wasn't. The same is true of the firm. Although you weren't content there, your feeling of disenchantment was more of a reaction to the past problems with your family than it was to the present and to the firm."

I stared at Dr. Ling and reflected on what he was telling me. I felt like I was seeing my life in a whole different light. It was like discovering a musical note in your favorite song for the first time. You may have been listening to the song all your life. But maybe you never noticed the note before because nobody ever pointed it out to you. I wondered if my marriage to anger was the right way to live my life. Dr. Ling interrupted my thoughts.

"And it sounds like you released some of that pent up anger that night in Venice."

"You could say that, maybe," I said.

"And it seems you learned, albeit unwittingly, from that night."

"How so?"

"If it weren't for that night, you wouldn't have left Los Angeles. You wouldn't have transferred from the state college in Los Angeles to the University of Chicago. In all likelihood, you would have just stayed there in your own cocoon, hanging with Frank, and getting farther down the line into Frank's dark world."

"Dark world?" I asked in disbelief. "Right." Dr. Ling nodded.

"Call it whatever you like," I said. "To me it's the bright side. It is the real side of life," I continued with some uncertainty.

"Because it was comfortable and you knew it," Dr. Ling pointed out. "The chaos, fear, and danger of that world were home to you."

"As it is to many people," I retorted. "Life is anarchy, Dr. Ling. You are healthy today and tomorrow discover you have cancer. There is no order to it."

"But happiness lies in persevering over this disorder you are referring to, not giving into it."

"Otherwise?" I asked.

"You will never be at peace. You'll keep thinking one escape or another is the silver bullet for your anger," he paused to look at me so as to emphasize the point. "You may fall into intense routine and order, like your dad did and like you did at the firm. Or you may try delving into booze and dope, thinking they are your salvation, like many others have before you," Dr. Ling continued. "And the list goes on and---"

"But I have tried to escape that world in L.A. by moving!" I interrupted sounding like I was pleading for approval from a father.

He just looked at me.

"I wanted to see who I was, what I was made of. I wanted to develop myself…I suppose that's why I left," I said, still pleading.

He kept looking at me as if he were evaluating whether I was telling the truth, or just telling him things he wanted to hear so that I could leave, go home, and smoke more. He looked out the window for a moment. The bright sun shone inside his old Quarter apartment. He looked back at me.

"Jack, I have so many patients who are afraid to leave the comfort of their cocoons.

They may be in an abusive relationship. But they won't leave."

"Why not?" I asked, eyebrows raised.

"The uncertainty frightens them, as it does with most people."

I thought back to Frank. He was more in tune with the dark and chaotic workings of life than many of the highly educated people I have met. Education seems to have blinded them to the way things work behind the scenes and outside the textbooks they have read.

"I guess I can see that," I said to Dr. Ling. "I think Frank is a lot like that."

"Yes, Jack." Dr. Ling gave me a short nod.

"And then there are others who kind of coast through life." He moved his hand like an airplane sailing through the sky without any effort. "They go from one thing to another without really challenging themselves. Rich parents, good school, job waiting for them out of school. Many of them want to explore the what if?"

"What do you mean?"

"What if I moved to New York to become a writer? What if I went to graduate school for art history to become a teacher? What if I told my parents that I am gay? But they don't. They just keep going. They never find out the answers to their questions," Dr. Ling shared.

"And I guess after that night, I owed it to Liam to stop sitting on my proverbial death bed, wondering, 'What if I left Los Angeles?' And yet, all along, I have had a nagging fear of failing and being a loser. What's behind that fear?"

"I would say it's about ego, Jack. We are afraid to fail or take risks because we are afraid of shattering the perfect idea we have of ourselves. We are afraid to find out that we are perhaps not all that we thought we were cracked up to be--at writing, teaching, cooking, being a banker, whatever it is."

"But isn't it better to find out who you are than to wonder?" I asked. "I think so, but many people don't. What do you think?"

"I think so." I shrugged. "But maybe I never would have thought that way if it weren't for Venice," I said uncertainly.

"As you saw from that night, you will find that the best opportunities for learning about yourself often occur when you unexpectedly encounter random strangers in unknown places."

"Like meeting an Armenian in a Turkish bath?" I smirked.

"Or like meeting a whore in church," he kidded. "But, seriously, Jack, rebirth often lies in the seemingly random, not in the linear routine."

"So routine is bad?"

"Oftentimes. I mean, you can learn through repetition, like when you practice an instrument. But there is no need to tap into that inner voice when you continue with a routine for too long," Dr. Ling said.

"Maybe that is why you see the best musicians often reinventing themselves so that they can never be pigeonholed as 'folk' or 'rock'?" I asked and paused to think about what Dr. Ling said.

He took another sip of tea.

"Come to think of it, I think that's true. I reinvented myself, in a way, when I traveled to Italy," I said reflectively. "I didn't speak Italian, didn't know one person there, and had never visited the country before," I concluded as I looked out Dr. Ling's window. "But, in a way, I merely found myself there."

"Well, our time is almost up here, Jack. I know you are moving back to New York soon."

"Next week." I looked back at him.

"Do me a favor." He stood up. I did too. He put his hand on my shoulder and looked into my eyes warmly.

"Of course," I responded.

"After you leave here, and as you get older, please think about all the things we have talked about. Reflect on the ways you have sought to answer your feelings of disenchantment, fear, and anger with one silver bullet after another, whether with the routine of law firm life or otherwise. And then think about where this search has gotten you."

"You mean where my search for *the* answer has gotten me?" I asked, emphasizing "the" the way you might say "*the* answer to one plus one is two."

"Yes." He nodded approvingly. "And write your journeys into a journal."

"Why?"

"Because that will enable you to find your answers."

I looked at him tearfully. I was not ready to leave him. I knew I would not see him again. Nonetheless, Dr. Ling looked at me with a confident smile. I did not feel worthy of it. I knew I had not really learned all I needed to learn from him. Maybe he thought I would learn what I needed to learn elsewhere. So he hugged me tightly and warmly, and I did the same to him.

"Thank you, Dr. Ling, for everything," I said as we embraced.

"It has been my pleasure, Jack," he said as he rubbed the back of my shoulder.

After I left Dr. Ling's office, I started writing in a journal. It chronicles my multiple attempts, before and after I saw Dr. Ling, to find the silver bullet that would cure me of my anger. My first attempt was with routine. That entry follows. I was 26 at the time.

PART II
IN SEARCH OF THE SILVER BULLET

(A) ROUTINE

CHAPTER 4
Goodbye Starbucks

As I calmly strolled through the narrow cobble stone streets of Naples, Italy, rows of t- shirts, underwear, socks, and bras were drying above, shrouding me from the pounding, midday Mediterranean sun.

Suddenly I heard furious screams.

"Hey, stop! Stop! Stop! Help! Shit, shit, shit . . . stop you sons-of-bitches!" two blond, Midwestern-looking college girls yelled as they ran past me toward the two dark-haired, Neapolitan teenagers who were speeding away on their moped. The boy sitting on the back of moped was holding two fanny packs. Nobody in the street paid any attention. The river of Naples did not stop for the two American backpackers. They had likely been walking through the street as though they were back in Madison, Wisconsin.

Fortunately, I blended in. I had a beard down past my chin and a milk chocolate tan. I wore black Supergas (Italian sneakers), cargo shorts, a white t-shirt, and black Persol sunglasses: No backpack; fanny pack; camera; flag, of any kind; fancy watch;

or map. Some Italians even came up to me and asked for directions.

While in Italy, I had escaped my stifling New York routine where every day I would wear the standard New York lawyer business attire: slacks, button-down shirt, black dress shoes, freshly shaven face, nice watch, and, sometimes, artsy black professor eyeglasses. I would usually get into work at 9:00 in the morning after getting my regular morning beverage, Starbucks coffee, from the first floor of the building. I'd spend the rest of the day by myself, eating lunch and dinner at my desk, which allowed me to bill more – that's why the firm paid for my food. During the week, I would get home around 11:00 p.m. and get ready to start the day over again. I usually worked at least one, and sometimes two, weekend days.

This illusion of order and structure seems to give comfort to many people, and I thought it would do the same for me. But this routine had turned New York, and life, into a one-lane highway that I was stuck on until death – at least that's the way I felt after September 11th. It reminded me of the path that my father had been on since Liam died.

So I got off the path and bought a one-way ticket to Rome. It was in Italy that I met my inner self, and heard that little voice from inside, for the first time.

CHAPTER 5

Hello Marcello And Nicola

As I walked by the ornate Trevi fountain, I saw a couple. They were sitting next to one another in the warm Roman sun, giggling, and drinking a 40-ounce bottle of Peroni beer.

With his dreadlocks and square professor glasses, the man was an outlier in Rome's stylized and yet sometimes staid society. His long, slender swimmer's body was nestled into the side of the fountain. His build resembled my brother Liam's, but it was not as buff. His eyes were Irish green, and he sported a patch of hair just below his bottom lip.

Tripping with his girlfriend seemed to be his pastime. A timeless, sandy-blond beauty, she stood about five foot seven. She sat next to him, showing off her old-baseball-glove brown eyes to passersby.

I saw them pass a small joint back and forth with a big dab of class. They dripped with the smell of grass. Dorky as it might have been, the Valley boy transplant in Rome was eager to partake.

"Si fa a parlare un po' Anglaise?" I asked the man, trying out the phrase for "Do you speak a little English?" as I approached them.

"Si, bene, un po' Anglaise," he said, meaning "Yes, good, a little English." We introduced ourselves in Italian.

"Mi chiamo Jack," I said to them.

"Ciao, Jack, mi chiamo Marcello Vivaldi," he said. "Eh, Jack, mi chiamo Nicola Vivaldi," she said.

With their long strands of hair flowing in the light Roman breeze, the married couple held out their hands to welcome me into their worlds. I felt at ease.

"A little smoke?" I asked with an eager grin. "Si, bene," Marcello answered.

He got to the point and handed over the joint. I took a large puff. As the smoke filled my lungs, my body relaxed. I passed the joint back to Marcello.

"Bene, Jack, bene. Iz a strong, no? Like eh splash of pepper in the eye, eh! Ah, ah, ah!" He laughed a pirate laugh. "Eh, you a here on et vacation?" Marcello asked.

"Yes, I stay in Trastevere, in hostel," I said, adopting the broken English of my new Italian friends. Trastevere is a quarter of Rome just over the Tiber River. It's filled with bookstores, cafes, and small quaint apartments.

"How a long you a stay?" Marcello asked. "I don't know," I shrugged.

"And you a live where in America?" he asked.

I took another hit of the joint he passed over and passed it back.

"I have been living in New York." I blew out the smoke into the air.

Italians from Parliament walked by. They all sported shiny Italian suits. Formal and normal, they seemed to be judging us for what we were doing with our day. I thought to myself:

perhaps I should be walking with one of them, instead of sitting here, wasting my life. Marcello interrupted my negative thoughts, "New York! Ah, New York." He patted me on the shoulder old-boy style. "Bene, Jack. Coma here, coma here, sita here," Marcello pointed to the spot next to him. "I love New York."

So I sat down on the ground without a frown, right in front of the crown of the fountain, with my two new Italian friends.

"Peroni?" Marcello offered some of the beer. I took a big swig. People passed by us throughout the day as we sat, smoked, and drank beer. Nobody paid us any mind. I soon discovered sitting and doing nothing on a warm summer day is not uncommon in Rome.

"Et, Jack," Marcello continued, "un amici, fiesta, un underground, tonight, you a come?" He patted me on the shoulder like it wasn't over.

I was sedated yet elated.

"Si, Jack, come, come, we have new American friend, it's a great, we have a fun tonight, okay?" Nicola said revealing a small tattoo on her right breast. She seemed endearing like Paula, Frank's girlfriend – sweet and tough when things got rough. I had enough of wondering whether I was a loser for leaving the big law firm, and my term in Italy had just begun. I was so ready for some fun.

"Ah, si, of course, I come!" I said looking at both of them as I put my hands up in a eureka-type moment.

"Okay," Marcello said, "we a meet a here at 10:00 tonight, okay, and then we a go."

"Bene," I said.

We left the fountain around 4:00 p.m.

CHAPTER 6

Preppies, Stoners, And Dealers

When I arrived at the fountain at 10:00 that night, I heard a loud voice say: "Ciao, Jack, Ciao, Ciao!" Italians use "ciao" interchangeably as hello and goodbye.

I turned around. Marcello and Nicola were walking towards me.

Marcello was now wearing old Diesel jeans, a black corduroy shirt, and black Converse high tops. Nicola had on a white linen summer dress, a worn Levi's jean jacket, and white Superga tennie shoes. When she got closer, I could tell she was wearing a perfume by Hermes called L'Eau D'Orange, which smells like sweet fresh oranges.

"We go, now, Jack, party, yes?" Marcello asked as he slapped my back. "A real Italian party, Jack, okay?"

"Andiamo," I responded. "Let's go."

I was wearing a white t-shirt, dark Levi's, and gray Superga shoes.

"Bene, bene, andiamo," Marcello responded as he waved me to follow his lead.

We left the spacious area around the Trevi fountain and headed back into the pretty, winding cobblestone streets. Pity that my Italian friends had never walked the cobblestone streets of Pirate's Alley in New Orleans.

"Fuma, Jack, fuma?" Marcello held out a small spliff as we headed down one of the small walkways leading out of the piazza.

"Si, bene, un fuma, un po' fuma." I nodded and took the joint as Nicola walked on. "We a like Italian Cheech and Chong with this smoking, eh?" He said.

He smirked, I smiled, and we filed into a line as we moved forward. Loud honks, laughter, and bursts of conversation surrounded us on the crowded streets. Beats of music came from several bars as we walked forward and onward into the unknown darkness. Bright lights welcomed us around 11:30 as we crossed the bridge over the Tiber River, took a sharp turn under the bridge, and went into a large abandoned storage space to see the teeth of Rome's underground. Chrome-colored stars shone brightly that night in spite of the city lights. Nights that summer were filled with river breezes that would make you shiver during the winter. We arrived at the club. It was a narrow venue, but there was still enough space for a slew of motley people – preppies, stoners, and dealers, among them.

Marcello and Nicola knew them all. "Ciao, ciao, Marcello!"

"Ciao, Mario, comme estai?" (How are you, Mario?)

Mario was a well-dressed Italian man of about 40 years old, wearing a black sport jacket, loafers with no socks, rocks on his fingers, and cologne that lingered.

"Ciao, Nicola, comme estai?"

"Ciao, Franchesca, comme estai?"

Franchesca was a brown-haired hippie of about 23 wearing a Pink Floyd t-shirt, torn Diesel jeans, black Converse high tops, and a small silver ring in her nose.

These greetings went on for a few minutes. Marcello and Nicola were part of the underground royalty in this city. As we walked into the venue, they introduced me to a sea of their friends. I began to see the city through their eyes.

Boom, boom, boom . . . thump, thump, thump . . . boom, boom, boom . . . thump, thump, thump, the music possessed the 20-foot-high room.

The people stood shoulder-to-shoulder, getting stoned in the room made of ancient stone. Prone to smoking marijuana with tobacco, the Italians created a potpourri of smoke, beer, lipstick, sweet smelling perfume, and laughter throughout the night and into the morning.

The sun blanketed the dark landscape when we finally left the club at five in the morning. We escaped up and over the bridge to an empty soccer field where we sat, drank more beer, and smoked more grass.

"Et, Jack, we go a home now, yes?" Nicola said in her soft voice as she slowly patted my back.

"Si, bene," I answered and nodded.

"We a go to taka the bus, okay?" she said. "Bene, Nicola, bene."

In the morning twilight, we walked through Villa Borghese, a massive green park in the middle of the city, full of fresh air, trees, grass, and flowers. With the powers of nature around us, we walked down a hill to the bus stop. We waited there for another hour and a half.

No bus came.

But it didn't matter. As I got to know Marcello and Nicola better, they schooled me on the value of certain routines.

CHAPTER 7

Tu Vuo Fa L'Americano

"Et, Marcello, what you do here in Roma?" I asked as we waited. "Eh, how you say, architettura."

"Architect?"

"Si." As he said that, he pointed to a nearby church. I didn't know what he meant until I saw where he lived.

"And you, Nicola?"

"School a," she responded. "Architettura."

"Okay, capisco," I said, understanding her.

"And you, Jack, in New York, what you a do?"

"Advocato," I responded, Italian for lawyer.

"A, bene, Jack, motto bene," Marcello responded. "Eh, what do you think about America, Marcello?"

"Bene. Et, but, et, I think that a America is a not as a cool as it used to be . . . its like a, how you say, fat Elvis, eh?"

He gave a Cheshire cat smirk.

"There is Italian song called 'Tu Vuo Fa L'Americano,'" Marcello continued, "It a translates to 'you want to be an American.' The song is a parodia, et, un parody. It makes et fun of et Italians who a imitate de American life, eh, by drinking a whiskey, smoking de Camel cigarettes, and listening to rock n' roll, but who a still live off parents' money."

"Trustafarians. We call them Trustafarians in the States."

"Okay, okay, like a Bob Marley with family money and a Harvard education, eh?" he said smiling.

"Exactly," I nodded. "They got money the old-fashioned way: their grandfather died."

"Eh?" He looked at me.

"Never mind," I said.

"Well, uh, eh, after the war, the American lifestyle was very sexy in southern Italy, but many did not a like dis because they like the tradizione, the tradition, of Italian life. They a think dis American way was passing phase," Marcello said in his broken English.

"And do you think it was a passing phase?" I asked.

"Si, a little. I mean now a America is more like Britain, no? It has become more like the British that the Americans used to a say they did not like – the rules, the intense routines, the big government, the corruption. Eh, American corporations et conglomerata, conglomerates, now are the rule, no? You a fit in to dis, or you a don't. But, eh, it a seems to me the times of Levi's, Converse, and the Americana individuality brand is no more – yes, exist, but all made in China!"

"So you don't think America is a cultural leader anymore?" I looked at him.

Suddenly, a group of pretty Italian women walked by us. They were wearing elegant scarves and dresses. It looked as if they had come from a wedding party. They were laughing joyously with one another. I had not a clue as to what they were saying, but Marcello and I looked at them for a moment as they walked by. As our stares moved away from the women, he turned his attention back towards me:

"Mais, si, Jack, si." He patted me on the back to assure me. "But I think that it has changed . . . people used to think of America as the place to take a risk, to go and make something, like in New York. Many Italians go to New York to make a better life. But, echo, listen, New York is a very expensive now, non? You have to have a lot of money to make a business in New York."

"This is true, Marcello," I nodded. "New York used to be more friendly to the entrepreneurs – it has become more difficult to maintain an individual identity, and easier to fall into the anonymous corporate routine."

"Si, exactly. And a part of de reason, non, is that there are so many large banks that have de power. No question American individuality is still something many a Italian love. But, et, oh, how you say . . . it is less a now, capisco?"

"Capisce, Marcello."

"It's like a religion here in Roma, et Jack. The church here is more powerful than the Mafia." He looked around to see if anybody was listening. "Et, if I have a choice, I take being priest over Mafioso; you can do anything while priest here, non?"

He patted me on my back like we were two old cowboys watching the sunset as we smoked the last cigarettes for the day.

"And de church make a life very difficult for you if they don't like you, if you a don't do what they say, fall into the routine the church wants, and they always try to stay in power. Eh, that is why they take de side of Mussolini, eh? To stay in power."

I agreed.

"I could see that from just visiting the Vatican the other day. I was amazed at the homage . . . "

"Homage?" Marcello interrupted.

"Respect," I answered and then continued. "I was amazed at the homage paid to all of the old priests who have passed – they are all in glorious glass, with their names on the front as a form of class, wearing their ostentatious gowns for all to see as tourists walk through the Vatican like sheep chewing on grass."

"Si, Jack, si," Marcello nodded. "Et, now a you understand, Jack," he patted me on the back, "but it is a bullshit, eh, because a the Church hide these a priests who touch the bambinos, nothing happens. Allora, many here routinely pay homage to the Church but a hate it."

"I totally understand," I said.

"And you, Jack, you have a family?"

"Yes, my parents live back in Los Angeles, my sister lives in France, and my brother died when he was 16."

"Eh, how?"

"Car accident."

"Oh, I am a sorry, Jack."

"Grazie."

"And how old was you?"

"10."

"Your parents must, eh, how you say, shocka?"

"Shocked."

"Si, shocked."

"They were, Marcello. My dad kind of escaped into a routine of work after the accident, whereas my mother at least faced it to some extent."

"Capisco," he looked at me with his deep green eyes, paused in thought for a moment, and then continued:

"I mean, routina is good to accomplish things, you know. It's is not a all bad, Jack. Maybe a your papa take it too far, the routine and all . . . but it takes disciplina to get a things done. And, eh, seeing friends, familia, a girlfriend, this a routine, is a good, you know, for you. For the a heart . . . I see my family every week, friends, and Nicola, it's a like water for my heart, dis routine . . . but, uh, eh, ecco, too much routine, I mean where you are trying to be like bird in sand, how you say?"

"Ostrich."

"Si, ostrich. If you a try to be ostrich with the a routine, then is not good for you. You lose sight of the choices in a life, you know. My father, who was polizia, he was too much into his worka, you know, that he don't a appreciate things." He drifted off, and Nicola softly yawned as we were all exhausted from the long night of drinking, smoking, and talking.

"Et, Jack, no bus. So we taka nap, eh, and then we a go to get soma coffee and manga, and then we taka the morning bus," Marcello said.

"Por que non?" I responded. ("Why not?" in Spanish.)

So we lay on the bus bench, got some shut-eye, woke up, and headed to the closest pastry shop for morning coffee, pastries, and Italian newspapers. After a while, we went back outside and picked up the next bus.

As I arrived at my bus stop, Marcello said:

"Et, Jack, you a come to stay with me and Nicola, okay? "No, I couldn't. I don't want to impose."

"It's no a problem, we want you to come Jack," Nicola said softly.

"Si, tuto bene, Jack. We meet you at 2:00 at the fountain this afternoon. Et a bring your things, okay?" Marcello insisted.

"Okay, grazie mele!" I thanked them.

I gave them kisses on both sides of the cheeks and left the bus. I walked back to my quiet, insignificant hostel. After I got there, I put my head on the paltry pillow as the comforting rays of Roman sun hit my face. Talking to Marcello about the benefits – and pitfalls – of routine triggered my memory of a session with Dr. Ling when I had told him about my father's worship of routine, especially of work, as a way to submerge the pain of Liam's death.

CHAPTER 8

Playboy Club Daddy

"My dad used to wear custom-made suits on a daily basis," I said to Dr. Ling as I looked out his window. The steamy New Orleans sunlight blanketed my face. I closed my eyes and started to act out my dad's actions, as though I were playing charades.

"He got his hair trimmed every week." I acted like I was slicking back my hair by pushing my right palm on my head and using my left hand to pretend to hold a comb.

"He wore the finest colognes." I patted my cheeks with my hands. "He always had nice Italian shoes or loafers." I pointed to my feet. I opened my eyes to look back towards Dr. Ling.

"His black Cadillac was always freshly polished." I made a polishing motion with my right hand.

"He sounds very dapper," Dr. Ling said as he sipped his tea. "And it sounds like he enjoyed cars, just as Frank did."

"You could say that," I nodded.

I looked back at him and kept reminiscing, this time with a happy smirk.

"My parents would often take my brother and me to the Playboy Club in Los Angeles to hear jazz and hang with the bunnies on Friday nights."

"The Playboy Club?" Dr. Ling asked with surprise.

"We had so much fun there," I said wistfully. "I remember my brother and I would fall asleep as the night went on, occasionally wakened by people laughing and the hot brunette, black, or blond bunnies smiling at us."

"I bet there were a lot of great musicians and comedians that you all saw there. I remember those clubs, like the one in New Orleans . . . they were known to be *avant garde*. Comedians like Lenny Bruce who couldn't really play elsewhere found a home at the Playboy Club."

"That's my memory of it. It seemed like an amazing place. It was a sign of the times in my family: hip, sophisticated, smart, loving, and loose."

"Just like your father used to be the Playboy Club daddy?"

"I think so. He was definitely avant-garde in a way too. He used to have gay friends when it wasn't cool to have gay friends. I remember that one of my father's main bankers, one who would fund a lot of his projects, was a gay man named Ray Bowen."

"His only friends were gay men?" Dr. Ling asked, smirking. "Maybe he wanted to play for the other team?" he asked with an even bigger smirk.

I looked back at him and appreciated the humor.

"No. I remember my father telling me about his black friends in Inglewood where he first moved with my grandmother when they left the Sheepshead Bay, Brooklyn, neighborhood. He told me how he would ride with them in his jet-black convertible Cadillac Eldorado when he was younger, and how they were continually pulled over because the cops thought they were pimps. I've seen pictures of them. They used to wear the kind of slim-fitting suits that are now in fashion. They were always with pretty women."

"And I gather your father's bravado changed after Liam died?" Dr. Ling asked.

"Totally. Just before Liam's death, my dad started remodeling our house. The floors were torn apart. Exposed concrete was everywhere. The kitchen was gutted."

"Did that continue after Liam's accident?"

"No. The renovation stopped. The house, as it stands, is somewhat of an eyesore on the block. It looks haunted. It makes me sad when I see it: cracks on the outer walls run from the ground upwards. Live wires hang from the roof in the front and dangle to the ground. Distress marks surround the garage door, and the inside is a barren wasteland. There is no carpet, no furniture, and no kitchen."

"How did you wash things?"

"In the bathtub."

Dr. Ling looked at me with sad, sympathetic eyes. I looked back at him the same way. "What did your father do to cope after Liam's accident?"

"He worked, and worked, and worked, and worked, and worked, and then worked some more."

"It sounds like he was trying to submerge his anger, guilt, and grief underneath the smooth waters of his work routine." Dr. Ling observed.

I didn't get what Dr. Ling was saying until I tried to do the same thing myself in New York City with my work life.

"Maybe," I said. "He would go to the office in the morning, attend meetings during the day, tend to his Cadillac, and then come home late at night."

"It sounds like he camouflaged his pain well at the start," Dr. Ling said, "but it became more visible as time went on."

"I guess so," I shrugged.

"But your mother's pain was more apparent from the start?"

"It seems like it, now that I think about it. She seemed to have grieved from the start. My father never grieved."

"This makes me think of the mom in the movie, *Ordinary People*. Did you ever see that?" Dr. Ling asked.

"I think so. Do you mean the one with Timothy Hutton? He loses his brother in a drowning accident on Lake Michigan, right? And he tries to commit suicide?"

"Exactly. In the movie, Hutton's character is seeing a psychiatrist played by Judd Hirsch."

"I remember that," I nodded.

"Do you remember a scene where the father, played by Donald Sutherland, tells someone at a posh, north-side Chicago party that Hutton was seeing a psychiatrist to deal with his problems?"

"Not really," I said.

"Well, in the scene the mom, who is played by Mary Tyler Moore, is ashamed. She even berates Sutherland for telling someone at the party about Hutton's psychiatrist."

"Why?" I asked. "Why was she so mad?"

"What do you think?" Dr. Ling asked.

I paused to think for a moment. I heard some southern Georgia-sounding tourists on the street talking. "Now whatch y'all doing tonight? There iz some good ole music up in, um, that neighborhood, I think it's called---" the man said.

"Frenchman Street," the woman said. "Says in this map here that's where the music is rolling."

And then my attention turned back to Dr. Ling's question. "From my recollection, the mom was very type A?"

"Yes," Dr. Ling nodded.

"She was a perfectionist," I added.

"She was." He nodded again. "There is status in appearing to be perfect, to always be stylish, have the right home, the right husband. The list goes on. So Hutton's imperfection, his inability to deal with the situation on his own, angered her. She wanted to close her eyes to him. She wanted to close her eyes to it all, really."

I listened intently to Dr. Ling as he continued, "There was a scene in the movie where she even gets mad at Hutton for being in the hospital after trying to commit suicide. 'Your brother wouldn't have been in there,' she said to him. And yet Hutton is the one who survived. He is the one who held onto the boat. He is the one who did not drown. He was, in the end, the stronger one."

"If I remember, his mom couldn't handle it," I said.

"Exactly," Dr. Ling said. "Instead of dealing with the fact that her son had died, she wanted to escape the fact by immersing herself in the routines of traveling, playing golf, and going shopping. By the end of the movie, she had to leave."

Dr. Ling paused to look at me. "Who does she resemble in your family, Jack?"

"She resembles my father?" I asked.

"Pretty much. He thinks he can cure himself. He thinks that seeing a psychiatrist is an admission that something is wrong with him. It is an admission that he needs the help of someone who is, in his view, a random stranger, to pull himself up by the bootstraps. It is, in short, a concession that his routines have failed him."

"And yet he was the one who suggested I see someone like you. It makes me angry that he won't take his own advice. He is so brilliant and such an amazing man."

I paused and Dr. Ling encouraged me, "Please go on, Jack. You are doing great." I looked at him and felt at ease.

"When he was younger, he got a scholarship to MIT, but he didn't go. My grandmother wanted him to make money so that is what he did. Plus, he has a very giving, warm heart, and yet he is throwing it all away." I paused and looked down towards the ground. "I am scared of turning out like him."

"If you didn't come to see someone like me, you would likely end up like your father.

You would be unwilling to love yourself because you aren't perfect."

I looked up at Dr. Ling, "That's what I am scared of," I said worriedly.

"Jack," he said, looking carefully into my eyes, "you decided to come here. Nobody forced you to. The biggest first step in addressing a problem, whether it is anger, depression, or addiction, is admitting that you <u>have</u> a problem. So please don't fret. You are here, and your presence is evidence enough that you are not your father. You are from him – but you are not him. You are Jack. Don't forget that."

I remember looking at him with a reassured smile. As my memories of this session with Dr. Ling faded, I got up from the glorified cot, put on my backpack, and went to meet Marcello and Nicola at the fountain.

CHAPTER 9

Italian Moonshine

Nervously shaking, baking in the sun, and pacing back and forth in front of the fountain, I waited for them. Would they like me there? Would I like it there? Weird that total strangers are hosting me like this? Marcello and Nicola picked me up at the fountain, and we took a taxi to his apartment, which was not too far from the Coliseum. I was still nervous as we rode, but Miss Rosella, Marcello's mother, made me feel better. When we arrived at the apartment in the early evening, she kissed me on both cheeks and gave me a warm hug.

"Ciao, Americano," Rosella Vivaldi, lightly greeted me, about five foot four, she had elegant, graying hair, a petite nose, and piercing blue eyes; she wore jeans, running shoes, a long cream linen shirt, and bracelets on her wrists.

"Ciao, ciao, mi chiamo Jack."

"Ciao, mi chiamo Rosella," she smiled a wise, 74-year-old smile.

"You a stay over here a," Marcello pointed to a spare, small room that smelled like fresh flowers with a pinch of patchouli. Tea simmered on the stove as I strode over to look into his room, filled with architect books. After a quick glance, I walked to my own room.

Lemon cello, a sort of Italian moonshine made at home with lemons and vodka, was on the table when I came out of my room. Candles were lit and the table had been set.

"Eh, Jack," Marcello came out of the kitchen, "dis is our routine, eh, to have nicea dinner with family or friends on Friday, okay?"

"Bene," I said, sat, and took a glass of the lemon cello. They did the same. "Salute," I said as I raised my glass.

"Salute," they all responded as they raised their glasses.

That night Rosella prepared an excellent meal of pasta, fresh tomato sauce, a salad, and Pinto Grigio. I tried with all my might not to drink too many glasses of the lemon cello. We all went to sleep early after dinner and awoke the next morning to make my plans to travel to Sicily over homemade pastries and fresh espresso Rosella prepared for us.

"We a know many a people around Italy, Jack," Marcello said smoking a cigarette as he sat at the table in his white tank top, "and we have many friends in Palermo. We a call them for you. They a pick you up from the train station, okay? You a tell us when you a go down, and we have them pick you a up, capisce?"

"Capisco."

I went online to purchase my train ticket for Naples, and then for Palermo. I gave the information to Marcello so that he could coordinate with his friends in Palermo.

"We a take you a to the train," Marcello said. "You don't need to," I said.

"We a want to, Jack, no problem."

So we all took the bus to the train station. They sent me off to my trip to the south, which included a stop in Naples, with kisses on each cheek.

"I see you a little bit, before I leave to go back to the states," I said. "Bene, Jack, bene," Marcello said as he kissed me on both cheeks.

I boarded the train. While I don't believe in labels, I soon discovered that Naples lived up to its reputation as one of the most dangerous cities in Italy; I had seen the American girls get robbed in broad daylight, but I hadn't realized the peril of Naples. With some trepidation I headed to Palermo, Sicily, where I wondered if there would be more danger and blight.

CHAPTER 10

Sicilian ZZ Top

A small two door red Fiat honked at me twice. The stocky 32-year-old man in the passenger seat sported a hillbilly beard that went down to his belly. I took my backpack from the storage bin and walked off the train into the powerful Sicilian sun, which is when I saw the Fiat's driver. The leaner and taller 33-year-old driver had a hillbilly beard, too. They were like Sicilian versions of the bearded ZZ Top band members in their music video, "She's Got Legs." It was about 11:00 in the morning.

"Eh, Jack, eh, Jack, vi, vi," I heard from the driver's seat as they called to me to come over.

I guessed this was my connection in Palermo that Marcello and Nicola told me about. As I approached the car, the driver, who was smoking what looked like black tar got out:

"Ciao, Jack, ciao, mi chiamo Giuseppe Vivaldi," he said, introducing himself, "but calling me the Pepe, okay?"

"Ciao, Pepe, ciao," I said.

Pepe then kissed me on both cheeks and gave me a short hug. Lugging my backpack into the small Fiat, I felt like I was traveling on a magic rug.

Beep! Beep! Beep! Ciao! Ciao! Ciao! Beep! Beep! Beep!

Sheep, buses, cars, mopeds, tourists, bags, kids, and sun surrounded me in the middle of Palermo. Flowing as the city did with espresso-induced speed, I wanted to drink in the Sicilian elixir.

"Ciao, Jack, mi chiamo Vito Vivaldi," the bearded passenger in the back seat said to me as I got into the car.

From what seemed afar, Vito leaned over from the back seat to give me a kiss on both cheeks. As I sat in the passenger seat, I felt beat. A neat, small hand reached over from the other back seat and planted itself on my left shoulder. It was the hand of an older, clean-shaven third host, Giacomo, who was also about 32.

His hand had a clear message: "You are in safe hands."

After I settled into the tiny red Fiat, we sped off into the slightly larger, labyrinthian streets of ancient Palermo. I had no idea where we were going.

"We a go to my house, eh Jack!" Pepe said as he drove the car smoking his tar. Bump . . . bump . . . smoke . . . bump . . . smoke . . . bump.

Every other street was a treat of potholes.

Every other street was also a meeting between Pepe's lips and his dark colored tobacco. Rows, rows, and rows of fiery red tomatoes surrounded us as we arrived at Pepe's house, which was situated smack dab in the middle of rolling mountains, cotton clouds, and plush green Sicilian grasses. As the Fiat toiled up the steep mountain, I saw the castle that was Pepe's house: Spanish tiled roof, two stories, stark white stucco, large fifteen-foot windows that felt at one with the mountains, and ancient wood beams. I was bursting at the seams to peak inside.

"Un café, Jack?" Pepe asked as we walked inside from the Spanish stone covered driveway.

"Si, prego," I nodded.

As I walked through the hallway entrance, I looked toward the 15-foot-high country ceilings and then around Pepe's eclectic living room. A zebra rug filled the middle of the floor.

Vintage brown couches that looked like they were from a Hemingway hunting safari orbited the rug. Large photos of lions, tigers, and hunting dogs were strewn across the endless walls. And then there was an ancient-looking photo of a distinguished looking Italian man with a large mustache dressed in a black tuxedo, white tie, and ruffled white tuxedo shirt. I wondered who this man was. From his kitchen, Pepe interrupted my thoughts:

"Eh, Jack, you a like sugar in a de coffee?"

"Si, prego," I answered.

I followed the aroma of the dark coffee into Pepe's massive kitchen filled with Boffi kitchen fixtures and 1920's Sicilian advertisements for olive oil on the walls.

"Here a you go, Jack. Coffee Sicilian . . . style," he handed me the small glass of steaming coffee while wearing his apron which read "Kiss me, I'm Irish."

With glee I took a sip and, immediately, my lips wanted to take another dip into the coffee.

"Dude, how did you make this stuff?" I asked Pepe.

"Ah, Americano, it is very simple: first – you a put fresh cold water into the bottom of the . . . how you say . . . Bialetti. Eh, echo, listen, and then, secondi, you a put de fresha espresso into a de bottom, and pound it in." He pushed his worn-looking farm hand down onto the coffee. "When de a coffee coma to the top a, you take a off the coffee from de heat, put little sugar, mix, and then you have it!'"

"Presto, just like that?" I asked.

"Si, Jack. Mange?" Pepe asked wondering if I were hungry.

I looked outside and saw that the boys were smoking their spliffs on the patio overlooking the vast mountain region outside. Boy, was I on some exciting ride.

"Si, prego," I nodded to Pepe. The sun took its daily nap, the moon awoke, and darkness shrouded the cool mountainside.

"Bene, you take uh, how you say, napa?" Pepe said. "Nap," I corrected him.

"Nap," he said with a grin as the sun light from outside grew increasingly dim.

Turning up the circular staircase that went to the second floor, I was looking forward to a good snore. Red tiles were under my feet led me to my room, the only one lit among the four or so bedrooms on the second floor. I fell on to the ancient, engraved wood bed like a heavy boar. As I peeled back the covers, I smelled the sweet smell of fresh lavender.

After the nap I felt like I was ready to rap when the clocked turned 10:00 p.m. When I came down the stairs, about ten or so men were at the dinner table trading stories, drinking wine, and looking fine. Some of the men had long wilderness beards, like my Sicilian ZZ Top hosts, whereas others had clean faces. Some men wore what looked like Kiton or Brioni Italian suits.

"Eh, Jack, coma down an a join us for our, how a you say, weekly dinner," Pepe said. He warmly waved his left hand for me to come over to their long fifteen-foot long table. I hate to label, but the dinner looked like something from the last supper. Generous portions of fish, salad, and several bottles of beer were on the table, not to mention about five bottles or so of Nero d'Avola, a local, hearty red Sicilian wine.

As I sat down next to Pepe, who was sitting at the head of the table, I asked him quietly: "Pepe, who are all of these people?" I said as I leaned over to his ear.

"They are amici . . . friends . . . from the neighborhood . . . they a come here every week for mange, to talk, and to share a stories, Jack," he said into my ear. "Some are a married, some are not, but all come to have a good time with the boys, eh?" He smirked and took a glass of the d'Avola in his hand to give me a toast.

"To the Americano!"

All of the men at the table raised their glasses. I was deeply touched that they made me feel like I was in the sunshine with them. That's because I was.

I thought to myself: maybe routine is not as bad as I thought it was before I took this trip? But I still couldn't get the idea out of my head of going to the office every day, at the same time, and leaving at the same time. I also couldn't get out of my head my father's routine: pounding his emotions into oblivion with the hammer of routine. Pepe interrupted my thoughts:

"Mange, mange, Jack. We have et coffee after . . . smoke some . . . and go to a club in Palermo, okay." Pepe heartily patted me on the back.

"Bene, Pepe, bene," I nodded.

Around 1:00 in the morning, I was reintroduced to the Vespas, small streets, and serious congestion in Palermo as our little crew went to some nightclubs and bars. There was not much dialogue between us. Their English was poor. My Italian was even worse. But it did not matter. Our actions expressed our affection more than our lack of words.

The next morning, we woke around 11:00 a.m. and went to swim in the Tyrrhenian Sea. The ocean made me want to see other parts of Sicily, so I booked a train for Cefalu, a small coastal village on the northern coast, about an hour away from Palermo.

After the boys took me to the train station in their Fiat, Pepe said to me as I left:

"Call us if you need anything . . . we a, how you say, here a for you, okay." He kissed me on both cheeks. "And a be a careful when you a travel in Sicilia. It a can be a very dangerous . . . but you a good at a keep a . . . how you say . . . low profile, eh?"

He smiled like he knew something that I didn't. I soon found out more about what he knew about Sicily and I didn't.

CHAPTER II

From Cefalu With Love

The 31-year old, five-foot-eight brown haired Sicilian woman with bright blond streaks wore a black bikini, had long athletic legs, sported large black Jackie Kennedy sunglasses, and had a red bandana wrapped around her head to keep her dirty-blond hair out of her face. I had read the Vikings came down to Sicily. I guessed she was from Viking stock. I continued to stare after the train let me off on the sun-drenched beach in Cefalu. She was scantily clad, lying about 30 feet from me. Italy was so good to me, and I wanted to be good to her.

So I then took a short nap. As I did, a voice said to me as I slept:

"Why don't you just jump off a high dive at night without knowing if there is water in the

pool?"

Whether you are a fool or a wise man, or both, we all have an inner self and a corresponding inner voice. Sometimes we rejoice when we hear that voice in a far-off, random land without anybody we know around where we stand. Without that band of friends to support you, the inner voice comes to you out of the blue.

My inner voice came to me during my dream on that beach in Sicily. Caring and yet steely, it spoke to me with grace. Since then, I have named my inner voice Ace.

His wrinkled face is that of an athletic, old-school, Dutch-English-Irish 75 year old. Standing about six feet with a shock of crystal white hair, he looked like an insurmountable wall. He stood tall wearing his crisp Savile Row single-breasted three-piece black tuxedo; black Tudor John Lobb boots; custom-made, white sea-island cotton tuxedo shirt; silver-cased pocket watch, the kind made by Stewart, Dawson & Co in Liverpool, with a gothic looking wolf's head on the chain; and an oval, white-gold, English signet ring on his left pinky.

Ace sat on a jet-black Chesterfield leather couch in my dream. He closed his book, marked his place, and took off his glasses:

"Sicilian families are notoriously protective of their women – and dangerous – even if you were Richard Gere. So you need to be careful." He stared at me through his round, clear, Anglo-American 1940's glasses, with his pale-rider blue eyes. His eyes calmed me like a cool glass of red wine.

In my dream, I was sitting across from Ace on a wooden Quaker chair in The Chicago Club library overlooking a vast Lake Michigan. Ace's creamy skin contrasted with Duke and Lila, two jet-black Labrador retrievers sitting on a charcoal-gray Persian rug next to his feet. I wouldn't have dared back-talk this serious looking but caring man.

The Sicilian sun beat down on my face when I awoke from my dream. I gathered up the courage to introduce myself to the Viking-Sicilian woman.

"Ciao, mi chiamo Jack," I said with the spirit of be-bop as I trotted up to her.

"Ciao, ciao, mi chiamo Bianca, Bianca Vivaldi," she thankfully answered as she lay there while I stood in somewhat of a lurch. "Americano?"

"Si," I nodded.

We shook hands.

I pointed down to the sand next to her. "Si, prego," she said.

I silently praised her as I gazed at her toned, tan legs. She slowly rubbed them together like a grasshopper while looking at the ocean.

"Tu parles ampu francais?" I asked her wondering if she spoke French.

"Qui, ampu," she answered, with a heavy Italian accent.

Little children played around us. Parents yelled at them in Italian to, no doubt, not get too close to the water. Lovers were also lying with one another careful not to smother. It was a family beach, after all.

"Tu habit en Cefalu?"

"Qui, j'habite la." I live there pointing to the little mountain. I looked over to it and saw the small, winding medieval roads dotted with apartments as clothing – shirts, pants, underwear, socks, bedding – hung outside for drying in the distance.

"C'est genial!" I said. That's great!

"Qui, et ma famille habite dans un petit ville a cote d'ici," she said, explaining that her family lived in a small town close to here. "Et tu?"

"Avant, j'habit en New York, mais, quant je revenir en Aux Etas Unis, j'espere que j'habit en Nouvelle Orelans, en Louisiane." Before, I lived in New York, but, after I come back from my trip, I would like to live in New Orleans.

"New York! Wow. C'est genial!" That's great!

Some of the children playing in the background splashed into the ocean and started screaming because of how cold it was.

"Mama, mama, mama!" I heard one child screaming and then looked back at Bianca. "Qui, c'est un ville manufique," I said as I looked at the children playing, "a la meme temps, je me manqué les temps plus tranquille and simple – comme ici." Yes, it is magnificent. At the same time, I miss the tranquil and simple times – like here.

"J'imagine," she agreed. "Mais, New York est un monde avec beaucoup de chois. Ici, c'est plus petit et il n'ya pas assez de chose pour faire. Donc, il faut que tu apprecie, non?" But New York is a world with many choices. Here, it is smaller and there aren't as many. So you should appreciate, don't you think?

"Mais, j'adore ici en Italy, Bianca." But I adore it here in Italy.

"C'est un bonne point, Bianca. Q'uest que tu fais pour diner? Tu veux rendevous avec mois a tout l'heure?" But that is a good point, Bianca. What are you doing for dinner? Do you want to meet with me later?

"Bene, Jack, bene, huite heure chez moi?" How about eight at my place?

"Super!" I was relieved as I closed my eyes again in thanks. She gave me her address and I felt a little stress.

"Sicilian families are notoriously protective," I remember Ace telling me in the dream. I worried: would I scream when they cut me if I slipped up?

To shut myself up, I packed my bag, went toward the local hostel, and took a step up to get closer to the tangerine-colored Sicilian sky. I took a shower at the hostel, felt like I had a little more power, and was off to the house of my Sicilian flower.

"Knock, knock," I knocked on her door like I was some medieval suitor. The door opened to a small and intimate apartment that was a love compartment – wood floors, ocean, paintings, worn leather couch, small kitchen fit for one person, and angel's breath flowers. Showers of garlic and tomato delighted my nose as I walked inside.

"Ciao, Americano," Bianca said.

"Ciao, Bianca," I kissed her on both cheeks.

"Come to my a place, okay? Maka a yourself at a, how you say, at a homa?"

"Yes," I smiled at her pronunciation, "at home." I felt right at home with the ocean breeze coming through the windows. I sat on the couch.

"Campari?" She asked.

"Si, grazie," I said with a nod. "Bene."

She brought over two Campari drinks with rocks and placed them on the coffee table. I sipped my drink as she continued cooking, intermittently coming over to take a sip of her drink.

"Howa you like a Sicilia, Jack?" she asked as she did her cooking almost without looking.

"I love it, Bianca, I totally dig it," I said as I sipped my drink. "The people, the beach, the mountains, the nature," I said looking out the small window. "It's like a California from the past, without all of the rules."

"Italian wild west?" she turned around to give me a flirty smile. "Exactly," I nodded with appreciation.

"Bene, Jack, bene," she turned back to finish her cooking. "Et finish, and now we mange, okay?" She started bringing dishes to the distressed wood table in her living room. I got up to help her. When we sat down, I poured her some of the white wine that was on the table and then poured myself some.

As we ate the garlic fish, and the breeze from the ocean wafted through the windows, Bianca said to me:

"Je veux trouve l'amour real. Je veux trouve un homme qui m'aime et qui je laime a la meme chose. Je veux vivre avec un amour tout les jours." I want to find real love. I want to find a man who loves me as much as I love him. I want to live with a love every day.

"Qui, je voudrais la meme chose," I agreed. I would like the same. "Je me souviens un fille qui je recontre a Nouvelle Orelans qui ma dit: tu meriter une fille qui tu meriter toi. Ca c'est bonne!" I recall a woman who I met in New Orleans who told me: you deserve someone who deserves you. This is good!

But then I quietly wondered: every day? Do any of us want real love every day? Doesn't the routine of it get too much to handle? Isn't that why so many couples fall apart? Isn't it because of the routine?

Bianca interrupted my neurotic thoughts as she cuddled in a crouch with her smooth legs next to me. With glee I could smell the faint scent of Bulgari green tea perfume on her slightly moist neck.

As the night went on, we gently cuddled. I left her apartment around ten, went back to my hostel, and met up with her again the next morning. As we drank our espressos, I took another jump off a high dive at night.

"Tu veux allez avec moi en Marseille? J'ai famille qui habiter la. Et je pense que t'aime rendevous avec moi après que je parti." Do you want to come with me to Marseille. I have family that lives there. I think you would like to rendevous with me there after I leave here.

"Qui, c'est genial, Jack. Je ne jamais allez au Marseille. C'est un bonne idée!" Yes, that's great. I have never been to Marseille. It's a good idea!

We then arranged for our flight to the south of France.

After our short flight into Marseille, my aunt came to pick us up from the airport. We wound through the small streets of the city until we exited on the main thoroughfare which kissed the ocean and arrived at my aunt's and uncle's house. Their backyard was full of flowers and little trees, and had a large table for entertaining. The warm Mediterranean sun was shining and spread itself over the backyard.

Bianca looked like she was going to a funeral -- black hair, black dress, black sandals, and light brown olive skin. While it is hot in Sicily during the summer, most Sicilian women wear black nonetheless. She did the same in Marseille.

She was stunning.

That night, we had a mix of fresh seafood and Pernod, a licorice tasting drink popular in the south of France, with my aunt and uncle.

The next morning, we took the train to Aix-en-Provence, a small town outside of Marseille full of flowers, sun, and small cobble stone streets. We bathed in the sunlight as we walked through the streets, holding hands, and soaking in the beauty surrounding the town. I had never met a woman like Bianca and haven't since. While this was the last time I would see her, she gave me hope that I would meet a woman like her again some day.

Of course, while I wanted to stay, I could not keep the beckoning call of Rome at bay.

CHAPTER 12

Whole Foods Organic Amnesia

Buzz, buzz, and buzz – I hit the buzzer for Marcello and Nicola's flat. "Pronto?" Dominco answered over the intercom.

"Ciao, Marcello, c'est Jack!" I said. "Ciao, Jack! Ciao!!!"

Buzz . . . the door to the building slowly opened . . . I climbed the stairs to their flat . . . and before I knew it, I felt Marcello's warm hands slowly wrap themselves around my back as he gave me a hug.

"Ah, bene, Jack, you a real Sicilian now, eh?"

With a Berkshire pork-chop wide grin on his face, I thought he knew exactly where the foot job took place.

"Si, si, tuto bene, Marcello," I said with a wry smirk.

After the greeting, Marcello, Nicola, and I started our meeting over fresh espresso. Because I was always on the go when I was down South, I had so many photos of Sicilian ZZ Top, the Sicilian countryside, and the sea that I could not stop my mouth.

We spent the day conversing, joking, and toking. I knew that this would likely be the last time I saw my friends, as I was to leave for Amsterdam the next day.

"We a take you a to the train for a your trip to Amsterdama, Jack?" Nicola asked with a sad face and a quiet voice.

"Si, prego," I responded as I felt her hand slowly come off my arm.

While crime is often done to the loving heart by the forgetful mind, I knew my heart would have a permanent scar after leaving them that day.

Slowly I fell asleep on the train to Amsterdam after my best Italian friends – or some of the best human beings I have ever met – left their American to move on to other lands.

During my nap, my anxious running mind was eager to ski downhill without order or any sense of routine as I dreamed:

"As you have seen from your travels in Italy and from the fine friends you have met, Jack, routine can be something that can protect you from the fear and uncertainty of tomorrow, like when you spend time with friends and loved ones," Ace said to me in my dream.

"Routine is mere deodorant," my angry, scared self responded, "people like these Italians try to cover up the smell of their humanity, their pain, their anger, just like my dad did after Liam died," I retorted to Ace without losing pace. "Unlike them, I want to be the gem that needs to feel the cold of *constant* uncertainty to feel what it means to be alive. I don't want to get close to anybody, and to do that I need to be the rolling stone that gathers no moss."

"Like being naked in a snow storm?" Ace asked in jest and responded next: "But sometimes you can lose your sense of self because you adapt too much."

"No," I said to Ace's face in the dream, "I need to adapt, adapt, adapt and adapt so that I can't recognize my self any longer," I retorted. "I want to forget about who I am, about Frank, and about that night in Venice Beach. The best way to do that is to get away from myself, to always be becoming someone else, moving somewhere else, and being with someone else. I never want to get close to anyone."

"Sounds like a Whole Foods organic version of amnesia."

"Gluten free," I said.

"Never forget who you are on the inside, Jack," the Claytonper and yet brooding sweet- and-sour tuxedoed Ace shot back.

In what seemed like a split second flat, I woke up from my long nap as the train was arriving in Amsterdam. It is there that I learned the wisdom of Ace's words.

(B) ADAPTATION

CHAPTER 13

Shush, Only A Short Smuggle

"It's such a short smuggle, Jack" the smuggler told me. "To France?" I asked. "What about getting pinched?"

"There ain't no chance," he pranced. "It's such a short smuggle!" he said again.

Sneaky Pete Lantz was a tall blond Dutch-German fellow of about 29 years who was super-mellow. He stood about five foot nine and had a long assembly line body.

"In Amsterdam, you can grow for self-consumption, you know, so I grow at many places," he pointed around the city with the speed of a small mouse you can't catch. We sat at a ratty wood Dutch table in the smoky coffee house. "This will come to California some day," he said to me, telling me how one of his ancestors, a coffee shop guy named Chip Lantz, used to live, smuggle, and make the best coffee in San Francisco during the 1800s.

He took a toke off his joint, and I quickly got the point. In walked some stunning blond Dutch women resting their long elegant arms on their beaus. I could have frozen right there and continued to stare, but I stopped:

"So you have people grow for you all over?" I asked Sneaky Pete.

He nodded as I prodded, and then he passed over the joint so as to anoint.

"Here," he said, "I know you have it in you. After a short brew, you take the product down to France in the back of a rental, where everybody raves about the product. Your work is virtual so you have the perfect cover and so nobody will discover!"

We left the coffee house shortly and walked next to the canals of the city. I started to feel sort of shitty.

"Pete, I need to go back to the hostel. Let me think about this for tonight, and I'll see you at the coffee shop tomorrow."

I slapped Sneaky Pete's hand and started walking back to the hostel, where I took a short nap. After I got up, I took a stroll and stumbled upon some California boys who told me what it is like to hear a plump man scream for his life.

CHAPTER 14

Plump Adolf Hitler Screams For His Life

"Smoke?" Kelly Francis asked as his jade eyes peered at me from the top of his tall slender frame.

I am sure he was a hit with the chicks. While he was lean as a rail, he was far from frail. No. Kelly looked more like he just got out of jail as he rocked Stussy black and white checked shorts, blue slip-on Vans, a tight white tank top, and long, streaked brown hair that went down to his shoulders. Because of the muscular boulders on his legs, he could have been pegged for the son of David Beckham.

"Sure, why not?" I said as I looked around.

Cool air abounded in the middle of the refreshing summer night. The stars were bright as a breeze slammed on my bare sandaled feet like it was a wall of sleet. Of course, it was no feat to find some coffee and smokes after I awoke from my nap at the hostel. And, of course, I passed what seemed like brothel upon brothel before sitting on a wooden bench next to one of the many placid canals that line the city.

Kelly and his brother Andy Francis, another California beach cat, sat down next to me. "Try this one. It'll rock your world." Kelly held out a joint with his long swimmer arm. I started taking a hit of the joint and then I got to the point:

"Where are you guys from?" And then I exhaled the smoke.

"San Francisco," Andy answered as I passed the joint to him. "And you?" he asked as he exhaled to pass the joint to Kelly.

"I live in New York . . . but I am originally from Los Angeles," I answered.

"I used to surf Rincon a lot when I was younger," Andy said. Trim and wearing a large, straw fedora, Andy was about six foot five, had long brown dread locks down to the middle of his back. Black Dickey shorts, brown Reef sandals, and a white tank top completed his outfit.

"Dude, we used to surf Rincon a lot together when we were young," Kelly chimed in after taking a lumberjack hit.

"That spot is top shelf," I said. "I used to go there when I was younger as well. I also loved hitting Trestles in San Clemente. "Good times and memories. So are you guys doing your post-college trip or something?"

"You got it," Andy said. "Berkeley?" I asked.

"I went to Cal," Andy said.

"And I went to Stanford," Kelly said as he exhaled his share of smoke, and then passed the joint back to me.

"Nice," I inhaled, "my sister went there, too," and then I exhaled. "What did you guys study?"

"Philosophy," Andy said. "Economics," Kelly said.

"I studied both," I said.

"Where did you go to school?" Kelly asked. "University of Chicago."

"Right on," Andy said, as he moved his long brown bangs out of his eyes, took the joint, and then took another hit to finish it off.

As we sat there watching the waves of Dutch people and tourists walk by, I felt as if we were three old men watching time go by. While man can't himself fly, it felt like we were on an island high in the sky. And then, as he looked onto the smooth waters of the canal, Andy asked:

"So do you really think there is something to race?" He started rolling another joint.

"It's all bullshit," Kelly said. "I mean, you remember that night we saw that crazy shit next to the canal?" He leaned over to look at Andy, who was focused on rolling a proper joint.

"You mean with the almost drowning?" Andy paused his rolling and looked over at Kelly, who was sitting to Andy's right.

"Dude . . . totally," Kelly nodded.

"Dudes . . . what, what happened?" I asked.

Andy finished rolling the spliff and let it rip. He passed it over to me. I took a nice toke and then gave it to Kelly.

As I did, a slew of Dutch locals who looked like professors of philosophy, art, or some other type of humanities rode their bikes by us. With their plaid jackets, black rim glasses, and book bags, they were deeply involved in what seemed like a stimulating talk. And then my attention went back to Kelly.

"I was walking down close to the canal," Kelly took a big hit, "and, all of a sudden . . . like a balloon popping," he slammed his hands together to make a big pop, "I saw this big ass white dude, I mean this guy was gigantic, who looked like a mix between Adolf fucking Hitler, cause dude's hair was super perfect parted and he rocked that shitty same mustache, and the fat guy who played that boss from the *Dukes of Hazard*. . . the, um . . . "

"You mean Boss Hog?" I asked.

"That's it!" Kelly snapped his fingers. "You know," he looked over to Andy, "the one who used to put a napkin under his chin," Kelly acted like he was putting a napkin under his chin, "when he would eat with Roscoe and the rest of his crew . . . bald on top, hair on the sides, and a large belly that hung over his pants," Kelly acted like he was pregnant.

"I remember him," Andy nodded. "I used to watch that show all the time . . . Daisy Duke was so fucking hot, dude . . . had a slamming body," he said as his eyes trailed a stunning brunette woman wearing tight jeans and a white t-shirt as she rode her bike next to the canal.

"Just keep passing the joint, dude," Andy said frustrated as he hit Kelly on the arm. "Well," Kelly handed the joint to Andy and looked back over towards me, "Boss Hog

dude with Adolf Hitler parted hair and budget mustache was in the canal screaming for his life . .

. 'Help me! Help me! Help me!' . . . as he made waves in the water."

"Were you scared?" I asked Kelly as I took the joint from Andy and took another hit to finish it off.

"So fucking scared . . . I didn't know what to do . . . I remember I just stood there with nothing to say . . . I just didn't know what to do," Kelly repeated like he was asking for forgiveness.

"I remember when that happened, man, far out stuff," Andy commented as he sat there. "And then I see this wiry black boy come out of nowhere and jump into the fucking

water!" Kelly continued.

Smack! Kelly claps his hands together hard. He got my attention.

"I mean, black dude was only a teenager," Kelly said, "but his arms were mad chiseled," he felt his arm to show how the kid was buff.

"Here, dude, take a hit of this shit," Andy said as he held out his freshly rolled joint.

I took a long drag off the stuff and, all of a sudden, my mind felt buff. I felt kind of tough sitting there with the guys smoking, and it was fun joking with them. I handed the joint to Kelly.

"Thanks, dude," Kelly said as he took it, took a toke, and handed it back to Andy. "And then what happened?" I asked.

"All I could see was some wrestling in the water," Kelly said.

"Dude, like two crocodiles in a mud match on a Discovery Channel show!" Andy smirked sarcastically as he handed the joint back to me.

Kelly ignored Andy.

"The thing is . . . I don't think that Boss Adolf Hitler Hog first understood what the boy was doing in the water . . . but then the Boss clung to the boy . . . it was so pretty to watch when the boy dragged the Boss out of the water," Kelly said with a soft tone.

"Yea, man," Andy looked at me, "we have had a pretty wild ride over here . . . we've had to adapt a lot along the way . . . things are so different out here than back home . . . things aren't always as they seem here."

"I bet," I agreed with Andy. "So what did you learn that night, Kelly, from the Boss Hog incident?"

CHAPTER 15

Filthy Rich Hollywood Producer

"What that night taught me," Kelly paused, "is to keep an adaptable mind." I took a hit off the joint and then passed it to Andy.

"You mean like Richard Simmons and shit," Andy said in his smart-ass tone, "have your mind stretch and do yoga and stuff like that?"

Kelly continued to talk as we all watched a beautiful, brunette Dutch woman with long legs, flowing hair, rich blue eyes, and a bright smile riding by on a bike:

"I mean, I don't mean to sound like some Benetton ad or something," Kelly looked at Andy and me, "but it just seems so odd how people often decide who they surround themselves with just by their covering," he shrugged his shoulders to express his uncertainty. "Boss dude maybe wouldn't have hung with that boy, but he saved Boss's life."

"Right on," Andy said. He passed the joint back to Kelly who took a long drag. He passed it to me and I took a hit.

"Yea, right on," I said, too, in a sort of dazed and confused tone. I passed the joint back to Kelly, he took another hit, and then he went on:

"I think that is one of the reasons I never joined a fraternity," Kelly continued. "Many of them seem to almost force you to hang out with a certain type of person, and even women at certain sororities as opposed to others, because they are chosen for you as being 'good.' And yet I found many of my friends adapting themselves so much to fit in with the crowd they were running with that they became different people."

"Like aliens," I said.

"I have seen that happen, too," Andy chimed in leaning over to look at us. "They get so far into adapting to the crowd," he pointed down into the water, "that you don't recognize who they are anymore . . . sometimes even *they* don't . . . and yet some of them remain open. What I mean is, that, um, some don't drink the cool aid."

"Or maybe the ones who 'lose themselves' were that person all along and didn't know it yet," I observed as I looked at both of them sitting on either side of me.

"Yea," Andy said, "maybe the person was predisposed all along to be like that, and discovered at that point that they did. It's like people who find out they are homosexual later in their lives when they are already married."

As he said this, three Dutch women (two blond, one light brunette) drove by on their black bikes. Their white linen dresses blew in the slight wind that came off the canal exposing their toned, supple thighs ever so slightly. They all sported black sunglasses of some sort or another – Ray Bans, Jackie-O's, cat-eyes. Their linen blouses opened up and showed their bare chests just above their breasts. As the wind moved through their long braids, they looked over at us, three California boys sitting there like nerds gazing at their beauty, much like we would gaze at a stunning wave breaking.

"Nice," Kelly said as he waved to the ladies, and as one waved back at us. "Nice is right," Andy agreed. "And they are for sure not fucking she-mans!"

"Right," Kelly said. "Organic . . . dude."

"Wow," I said in kind of lame amazement.

After the ladies went by us, we went back to our conversation like one would return to work after catching a glorious wave. And yet the conversation wasn't work for us. It was an exchange that helped me question whether my worship of adaptation at the time, after my trip to Italy, was the right path. We all paused for a moment after seeing the women, and then Andy lit up another joint, took a hit, and then passed it over to me. These were ideas I was wrestling with, just as many of us do when we are part of a large organization, a law firm, a bank, an advertising firm, or even a hippy movement:

"But those folks, I would think, would have already felt the urge when they were younger when exposed to the desired object – man or woman," I pointed out.

"Regardless of how you cut it," Kelly said, as he took a hit off the joint, "some may get married out of societal pressure when, all along, they have a latent desire to be with the same sex . . . but they suppress it to fit in to the group . . . just like many I have seen in school who try to act so cool in the Greek system."

"The thing is, Kelly, that happens in any large group," I pointed out, "whether it be a corporation, law firm, or hippy sect," taking another drag off the joint.

"Right, dude, right," Kelly said. "You really have to be adaptable or flexible so as to not be too rigid in your thinking as to who is and who is not good."

"Yea, dude," Andy chimed in, "but, you know, sometimes if you are <u>too</u> adaptable, then you don't have any consistent standards. *That* doesn't seem to be good either because *you* of lose your sense of self, or never allow yourself to develop it."

"All I am saying is that it is good to keep an open mind as to who will or will not fit your standards, not whether you should have standards," Kelly said.

"You mean like when parents approve of their daughter's fiancé even though he may be a coke fiend, or they may have suspicions that he is a coke fiend, as long as he is a filthy rich Hollywood producer! It's like that makes it acceptable, you know, for some people," Andy said.

"Exactly! Perhaps the daughter would be better being with a high school football coach who has a lot less money than the coke lad but who will be a good partner and father," Kelly agreed.

"Right, right on, Kelly," Andy agreed.

"Guys, I am so high . . . I had better say bye," I said.

"All good, Jack," Kelly said. He held out his fist to mine for a pound, and I formed a fist to pound his. I did the same with Andy.

"Safe travels, guys," I said.

"Totally, and you, too, Jack," Andy said. I went back to the hostel for the night.

Ace, my annoying inner voice, bugged me again in my dream.

"Learn from your experiences, Jack. To do that, you can't just forget about yourself and always adapt. Because then you are constantly reinventing who you are and making the same mistakes over and over again."

"But isn't adapting good?" I asked him.

"Of course it is," he answered, "that is how you survive. By adapting to the environment in which you find yourself. But, as the California boys pointed out, or as you learned from the giant goddess," he smirked, "don't adapt so much that you lose your sense of self, or who you are."

"So, how do I get the right balance?"

"Between?" he asked with his head cocked to the side.

"Routine and spontaneity, order and anarchy, structure and creativity?" Ace responded:

"You'll find your answers, Jack, as long you keep learning from the strangers you meet and experiences you have. Each person you come across can be like one of the books you read while at Chicago. They are there for you to explore and learn from."

Then I awoke from my deep sleep, feeling like a freak, and thought to myself: No way am I going back to meet Sneaky Pete. And then I thought: all life about is luck. No matter what I do, how much I try, or who I am, destiny has the answer for me.

(C) LUCK

CHAPTER 16

South Side Clayton

"Aren't you the former journalist?" I asked Clayton. He looked at me like I smoked crack.

I unexpectedly met Clayton Black on a sunny, spring Saturday morning in the lobby of the University of Chicago's International House (I-House). The I-House is a 1932 gothic dormitory for students and visitors from all over the world, including people like Clayton, a Yale graduate, and myself. After arriving back from my trip overseas and staying with Frank for a short stint in Los Angeles, I moved back to New Orleans. When I was 32, I moved back to New York City. During that summer, I went back to Chicago for alumni weekend.

"The one who was in charge of the journalists who stormed Normandy Beach?" I asked.

"Yes," Clayton answered, "how did you know?" He looked at me askance. I felt like, maybe, I didn't have a chance to connect with him.

"I was at the presentation yesterday by Steven Levitt . . . you told the audience who you were when you asked your question. I looked you up afterwards."

"Oh, yes, that's right," Clayton answered. "What year did you graduate?" he asked me. "1997," I answered.

"That means I have 60 years on you. I graduated, I can't believe it now, in 1937! I am a living dinosaur, eh?" he said in jest. I thought Clayton was the best!

Clayton stood about five foot seven and wore a blue seersucker suit and a white linen button-down shirt. His brown suede Clark shoes complemented his wrinkled old English ivory skin, sugar-white hair and goatee. His blue Swatch peeked out from under his left sleeve. I was also wearing a blue seersucker suit and had a blue Swatch on my left wrist.

"What is your name?" he asked as he held out his wrinkled hand in the sometimes scholarly, often dangerous, South Side of Chicago.

"Jack," I shook his firm hand.

"So, how did you like Chicago?" Clayton asked as he watched the flow of international people pass us by.

"I loved it. It was such a treat. Especially from where I came from."

"Which is where?" He looked over at me. "Minsk?" He smiled in jest.

"A state school in California. I had horrible grades in high school; I was such a fool, so I barely made it out of the pool of applicants to the state school."

No. I didn't tell him about my Playboy club daddy or the dangling, live wires in my concrete,

Addams Family home. Nor did I tell him about being mentored by the likes of Frank White growing up. But that is what I was referring to when I said: "where I came from."

"And then you transferred?" He tilted his head in intrigue. "Right," I nodded slightly.

"What did you study at Chicago?" he asked with a curious tone. "Philosophy and economics."

"Well, it's good to have knowledge of both numbers and humans. Otherwise, you get a narrow view of the world. You end up thinking the numbers say it all, or that people do," he said looking back towards the front door again and to the sun streaming in from the outside.

"Agreed," I said with a smirk.

"You must have been recruited by banks and other financial institutions after graduating?" He looked back at me.

"Totally. They recruited on campus." I nodded and crossed my arms feeling defensive about not going the banking route.

"Did you go that route?"

"No."

"So what do you do now?"

"I practice law in New York City. And you?"

"I have been a journalist for over 40 years, and I can't believe it has been that long." He looked down at the ground for a brief moment.

"Wow, you must have seen a lot during those years," I uncrossed my arms with relief that he wasn't judging me.

"I have," he nodded reflectively, "but maybe not as much as some of my other family members, such as a cousin of mine named 'Winston Black,' who I heard was a spy during WWII."

"He sounds like an interesting lad. What are some highlights from your life?" I asked him.

"Well, let me see." He paused.

"Overseeing the journalists that stormed Normandy Beach on D-Day."

I looked at him in amazement. I knew he had done that, but it was another thing to hear him say it. I felt like he was a trapeze artist who was able to fly over the Grand Canyon in one fell swoop.

"I read *The Longest Day* when I was younger."

"The book by Cornelius Ryan?"

"Right," I nodded. "So, during your career, I bet you have written about different characters?"

"Too many to mention," he nodded his head in disbelief as though he used to be a thief. "Who were some of the highlights?" I asked with anticipation.

He paused and looked at the walls full of black and white photos of former students and professors from Chicago dating back to the early 1800s. As he looked at the photos, he said softly:

"Well, let me see . . . Ernest Hemingway . . . um . . . Ingrid Bergman . . . uh . . . Robert Capa . . . uh . . . .Lee Miller . . . Henri Cartier-Bresson, are some." He looked back at me. "Quite a list?" he said.

"Yes," I nodded. "And now you are retired?" I asked him.

"In so many words, yes. But I stay active. I relocated to Paris and I stay appropriately active there."

"What do you mean?"

"I mean making good use of my time . . . not doing too much . . . not doing too little . . . having that right balance between the two is key."

"And tough," I said.

"No question," he nodded in agreement. "So why are you here if you live in Paris?"

"I often come to Chicago to use the libraries for research." As Clayton said this, he looked outside again as though he had somewhere to go.

"Impressive! Well, I don't mean to keep you," I said.

"You aren't keeping me at all. I just want to get outside into that lovely weather."

"I understand. I am about to do the same thing. It was nice to meet you, Clayton."

"Likewise," he said as he held out his hand. I shook it with a content smile.

Clayton and I parted ways in the lobby of I-House. When I got outside, the sun was shining and the Lake Michigan wind brushed against my face as I picked up my pace. I took a left outside I-House, walked down the tree-lined street of Kimbark Avenue, and then onto 57th Street. It has a number of bookstores and houses that were built in the 1940s.

CHAPTER 17

No Contract, Just A Handshake

"Well, hello again, Clayton."

"Hello, Jack!" Clayton said with a wry smile.

Coincidence or destiny I know not, but I got a second chance to speak to Clayton on the corner. I approached him, put my hand softly on his shoulder, and offered:

"Want to go to breakfast?"

"That sounds lovely. How about Medici?" he asked.

Medici is a Hyde Park restaurant on 57th Street frequented by local academics, neighborhood folks, and President Obama when he was lecturing at Chicago's law school.

"Let's," I answered.

As we started walking toward Medici underneath the canopy of trees that lined the street, Clayton bobbled back and forth like some creaky old boat riding rough waters. With his left hand on my shoulder he said:

"I walk like I have had a few drinks, eh?"

"Not at all."

It was a white lie.

"But it is really because of old age," he said. I smiled as we continued walking forward.

I picked up on Clayton 's thick South Chicago accent. He pronounced "car" like "caarrr," or "bears" like "bers." When I heard it, I thought about all of the tough figures who came from Chicago, especially the South Side, with its history of bootlegging.

"Are you from the South Side?" I asked Clayton. "Is it that obvious?"

"Well, your accent isn't that strong, but it is still noticeable. Are you from this neighborhood?" I pointed around us.

"Yes, I grew up in Hyde Park," he nodded as we walked.

"It must be nice for you to come back here after all these years," I said.

"These houses remind me of a period," he said as he looked around, "but I am afraid that period is now gone."

A group of six or seven smiling children ran passed us as they played hide and go seek, and one of them screamed back to their friend, "You're it!"

"What do you mean?" I asked Clayton as our eyes turned from watching the cute children back to the path in front of us.

"It was a period when men wore fedoras, when people dressed up when they left the house, and when there seemed to be less moral relativism."

A tall, bearded professor walked past us. He lugged a sack of books from the Seminary Co-Op, a local bookstore to, no doubt, do some research for some paper he was writing. He looked at us as we walked by him.

"Moral relativism? You mean the idea that morality can change with the whims and ideas of people?"

"Precisely," he nodded.

"How was it different then, in your view?"

"Well," he cocked his head and put his hands behind his back, interlocking his finger., "There seemed to be an idea of right and wrong. I feel as though people have more skepticism now toward the government, toward one another, and toward the world in general," he said straightening back up.

"What do you think caused that to happen?" I asked.

I looked back towards the partially cracked sidewalk in front of us. Beautiful brick homes were all around us with ivy climbing their walls and arched windows allowing the bright Chicago light inside. The old bookshelves beamed with pride in the sun, and so did the wood floors that were covered with Persian rugs and others from all over the world.

"Many things, including, surprisingly, prohibition," he responded and looked over to me. "Prohibition?" I asked with surprise.

"I think it made people resent the federal government." He looked back toward the sidewalk we were walking on. "A law was passed that only a minority of the population wanted," pushing his right palm out so as to emphasize the point. "The government said one thing, and did another. Police put people in jail for drinking, and then went home to have a drink themselves!" he smirked.

I then confessed to Clayton:

"These houses are old and not as polished as the new developments elsewhere. Yet I feel more comfortable with them. I feel like I know what I am getting with these houses. They are what they are," I said as I looked around street we were walking on.

"Things were more that way in the past, Jack," he said patting me softly on the back. "It wasn't as easy to camouflage things with technology. Business was done on a handshake – no social media apps, smart contracts, none of this modern malarkey. You often had to meet people in person to get anywhere. Yes, things are more efficient now. But there are costs to that efficiency," Clayton observed.

"We are both lucky and unlucky to have it all at our disposal, I guess?"

He nodded in agreement.

"All of this technology makes things easier but it also alienates people more than they realize," Clayton said.

As we walked down the street, Clayton and I almost looked like a grandfather and grandson duo with our blue Swatches, although I had a lighter complexion, Italian or even black Irish looking, with brown hair and broad shoulders. I was looking forward to getting to Medici. I had so many questions for Clayton. He was from a dying generation.

CHAPTER 18

Bigger Better Deal

We arrived at Medici and sat down. A waitress came up to us: "Good afternoon, gentlemen. What'll you have?"

The waitress was heavy set, with a nose ring, some tattoos on her arms, and dyed red hair that was pulled back into a 1950's bun. She had her pen and paper ready.

"Good afternoon," Clayton answered. "I'll have an orange juice."

"I'll have one, too."

"Anything to eat?" She asked.

"I'll have two egg whites with some wheat toast, please." I could tell Clayton liked being in places like this. He was an old teenager.

"I'll have the same, please."

"Very well," the waitress said. She wrote down our orders in the book.

Medici was full of writings scribbled on its wooden walls and booths. There is rooftop where you can sit outside underneath the trees and eat. We sat downstairs. It is a little dark down there, like a cave, but that is part of Medici's charm. Natives of the South Side worked there side by side with students from Chicago. I myself had been a bike messenger during my time at the school, but thought of working at this eclectic place full of local dealers, disc jockeys, jocks, nerds, professors, parents, children, and North Side residents visiting the edgy South Side. It reminded me of a more intellectual version of the underground club I went to that one night in Rome. The ceilings of the place were about fifteen feet high, and black and white photos of various people donned the walls. The place had a very quirky and yet very traditional vibe and felt very, well, hip libertarian.

"But you'll have to squeeze the orange juice for yourself," she said as she pointed over to the juicer and walked away.

Clayton leaned over to me and quietly whispered:

"I think I would have trouble squeezing mine," he patted my shoulder softly. "Can you squeeze it for me, please?"

Clayton's hand trembled as he struggled to bring his glass of water to his lips. So I happily complied with his request. After I squeezed our two orange juices, I sat back down with Clayton .

Clayton said to me, "You seem to have a good pulse on the old school."

"My dad spent some time growing up in Brooklyn during the war. So he has certain ways that are not as common now."

"And your career? How have you liked what you have been doing?"

"So far, I have been unhappy doing it. For my first two years out of law school, I worked at a large and prominent New York law firm."

"But you must have been making good money," he said as he sipped his orange juice. "Totally," I nodded. "I was likely making more money there than many of your

generation would make in four years, even adjusting for inflation," I said with a serious tone.

"So you had security?" he asked with raised eyebrows. "I thought so." I took a sip of my orange juice.

As I did, a motley crew of chemistry and physics students came in. A Chinese boy wore a shirt that said "Rational Geographic;" the Russian boy wore a Slayer shirt; and the Indian girl wore a t-shirt that read prominently: "For sure where fun comes to die," a reference to Chicago's reputation for being a hard-nosed academic training ground. The Indian girl was saying passionately to the Russian: "Yuri, the curve can't look that way. It would need to look this way," as she curved her hand in a mathematical graph manner, "in order to accurately track the trajectory of the atom." I looked over to the students and looked back at Clayton, who was waiting for my answer.

"After all, my 401(k) was booming. I had health insurance. I had a great loft in SoHo, a trendy neighborhood in New York."

"So life was, objectively speaking, splendid, right?" Clayton asked with a smirk that betrayed his rhetorical question.

At that point, the waitress came with our food and placed it on the table in front of us. I put some hot sauce on mine, and Clayton put pepper on his. As he took a bite of his dish, I continued:

"Yes, but, for some reason, I was miserable." I took a bite of my eggs. "Why?" Clayton asked.

"I guess I didn't want to end up like the partners at the firm." I took another bite and then paused as I looked around the room, and Clayton took another bite of his eggs.

Clayton interrupted my thoughts after he finished his bite:

"Why not? They must have been very successful?" he smirked.

"No question," I nodded. "There are reports the head partners were making something like $10,000,000.00 a year in cash."

"And, so?"

"But most of them were unhappy," I looked at him and paused to let it sink in. "They married and divorced in a New York nanosecond. They would stay at work during all times of the day, would often have mistresses, or at least talk about having a mistress. This would usually occur when the new crop of paralegals would enter the fray."

"But many weren't that way, right?" he said in a Devil's advocate tone.

"I shrugged with uncertainty." I pushed my egg onto the bread, "I actually think one of the head guys was a Bronx straight shooter in that realm. He fought in World War II. He was married to the same woman for many years. But other were not like him." I ate the egg and bread.

Clayton put his utensils down on the table and wiped his face.

"Jack, that doesn't happen only in law firms – it is pretty rampant, especially in big cities like New York," he astutely pointed out. "Some people are on a constant look out for the bigger, better deal. And so some people never feel at ease or happy with their choices. I would go so far as to say that parts of society are heading that way."

When Clayton said this, I questioned my immature outlook – and how much of it was tainted by 9/11. I also thought Clayton had some secret to share with me as to how he was able to survive and thrive this long, and yet keep to his old school ways. But I refrained from asking. I did not want to seem so forward.

"How do you like living in Paris?" I asked him.

He picked up his utensils, put a piece of egg onto his bread, and ate it. He then answered: "I love Paris. I couldn't live anywhere else. I live in a loft in the Le Marais district."

"If I recall correctly, that is the Fourth Arrondissement of Paris, which was traditionally the Jewish quarter?" I sipped my orange juice.

"Right," he nodded.

"I think that is one of the oldest neighborhoods in Paris. Now, it's full of artists and writers of all different stripes, in addition to boutiques."

"That is why I live there. The small streets, the cafes, the restaurants, and the people are invigorating."

All I could picture in my head was this white-haired, 80-year-old American from the South Side of

Chicago living somewhat like a rock star in Paris. Clayton told me he often had parties in his loft space where he would show his guests movies.

"How did you meet so many people in Paris?" I asked him with amazement.

"I was the head of the Democratic Party in Paris for ex-patriots. I met a number of people through the group."

"You are a lucky man, Clayton."

"Well, yes, I in a way am very lucky," he continued cautiously. "I'd like to keep in touch with you," I said.

"Take down my e-mail address. That is the best way to get in touch with me."

"I'll e-mail you later, Clayton, for sure." I wrote down his e-mail address on a paper napkin.

"I'll have to be moving along here, Jack. I intend on visiting the former dean of Chicago at Rockefeller Chapel."

"No problem. Let's get the check."

After settling up, we left Medici. Since I knew I probably wouldn't see Clayton again, I needed to ask him now for his secret of success. What allowed him to keep going all of these years? Where did he get his energy to live in Paris, commute to Chicago, and have all of those parties he was having back in France? Was luck the answer?

CHAPTER 19

Clayton's Secret For Success

When Clayton and I left the darkness of the Medici, the South Side sun shone on our faces. We headed towards the Rockefeller Chapel. As we did, Clayton asked:

"Are you married?"

He looked over to me and then looked back in front of him as he waited for the answer. "No. How about you, Clayton?" I looked over at him.

"No."

He paused.

"But I have been married three times."

"Three times?" I said in surprise.

We arrived at Woodlawn Avenue, which is one of the main stretches in Hyde Park. The street is full of grand brick homes and large trees that cover the middle of the street. We took a left and headed south towards the Chapel.

"Yes," he nodded. "My third wife died a few years ago." He looked over at me with sad, worn eyes. They were the type of eyes you have when you have a snowball day, week, month, year, or lifetime:

when your parents die, your lover dies, your children die, and then you find out you have cancer. His eyes were that kind of eyes.

"And before that?" I carefully asked. "My previous two also died."

I paused to take that in and process it. "That must have hurt you," I said.

"To say the least, Jack. So that is why I said that, in a way, I have been very lucky. I am still here walking next to you."

He paused to turn towards me and smiled.

"But, in a way, I have also been very unlucky," he turned to look straight ahead. "How do you do it, Clayton?" I asked in a curious tone.

"Do what?" he asked with surprise, like he didn't deserve the question being asked. "Survive such heartache?"

We paused for a moment at the stoplight. We were coming up to 57th Street, a few blocks from the chapel. As we walked across the block, Clayton asked me:

"Why do you ask?"

"I lost my brother in a car accident when I was 10."

"I bet that destroyed your family," he looked over at me then back towards the sidewalk. "No question," I paused. "I think it also made me very angry," I said as I looked up at the grand trees. I looked back towards him. "Those feelings caused me to get into a lot of trouble when I was younger, and I still have some of them lingering inside." I looked back to the sidewalk as I thought about the events of that night.

"I am sorry to hear that you are feeling so unsettled, Jack," he patted me on the back. "So I gather you, like many in your generation, are on a quest?"

"A quest?"

"Yes. You are on a quest for meaning in today's world. It is more maze like and less predictable than the one I grew up in," he looked towards me.

I listened as he spoke and just kept looking forward.

"A related quest of yours," Clayton continued, "it seems to me, young man, is how you can grow in a beneficial way from whatever trouble you got into when you were younger, rather than get stuck in it which is easy to do," Clayton said.

I looked over in surprise at Clayton's observations.

"I think so, Clayton. I mean why is it that some people move forward whereas other get stuck in their lives?" I asked.

"We know some of it is biology. Some people are predisposed to get stuck because they have a familial history of depression," Clayton astutely pointed out. "They are, in other words, born with the deck stacked against them."

"That is some people," I said. "In any event, the mind often affects the body, not the other way around."

"This is true," he conceded.

"So biology is not necessarily the answer. It just seems that some people are mentally better able to deal with imperfection, death, and the like, whereas other people seem to go deeper and deeper into all of those issues until they can't stop thinking about them."

"Like your dad?" Clayton asked as he looked over towards me. I paused.

"Why do you say that?" I asked.

"I kind of sensed it from what you told me about him. Sometimes people from that generation are too rigid. I can only imagine what he was like after you brother died."

"And you?" I looked over to him anticipating his answer.

"You mean you want my secret for success?" Clayton smirked. "The silver bullet." Clayton made an even bigger grin.

I appreciated his humor. We continued to walk down Woodlawn Avenue, surrounded by trees, gothic towers, and the 1940s houses. We paused for a few seconds, and then he interrupted the silence.

"There is no secret recipe, Jack," he put his left hand softly on my shoulder as we walked. "At least a kind of equation?" I looked at him playfully.

"I wish I could give you an algorithm." He paused. And then:

"I think I've just been plain lucky. Nothing more, nothing less," he said with a smile as he looked at me.

"That's all?" I asked in surprise. "Luck?"

"I didn't smoke, either," he said with a wry grin, as though he weren't divulging all he knew.

We walked by the Oriental Institute about a block from the Chapel, the home of the Chicago archeologist on whom the Indiana Jones character is loosely based. I thought of how Dr. Jones would react to my anticlimactic finding.

"But what is luck, Clayton?" I asked.

"I suppose another word for it may be fate," he said as we crossed the street to head toward the towering Chapel. On an overcast day, it looks like it could be from a Dracula movie because of its antiquated gothic features. "I mean, when I was younger, I had only been exposed to the Western view of prosperity." He looked over his shoulder to make sure no cars were coming. I did the same, and then I asked:

"Which is?"

"Lift yourself up by your own bootstraps to get you where you want to go in your life," he looked at me deadpan.

"And after?" I asked in suspense.

"I became more in tune with the Eastern view of life as I became older," he said looking up at the Chapel in quiet admiration.

"And that is?" I asked.

"Each of us is a candle with its own burning life." He looked over at me again with his deadpan look. "Oftentimes, regardless of how much you try, you cannot control when your candle goes out."

"But you do have a certain amount of control over your life and where it goes, don't you think?" I said with hope.

"Let me put it this way," he said as we were approaching the 15-foot wooden medieval door to Rockefeller Chapel.

"You applied to Chicago, right?" he asked just as we stopped in front of the towering door.

"Yup," I nodded.

"And you got in?" He put his wrinkled right hand softly on my shoulder. "Yup," I nodded.

"Had you never applied, you would never have known if you would have been accepted," he looked at me straight in the eye.

"No question," I nodded.

"But you weren't certain you were going to get in once you did apply?" he persisted. "Of course not. That's why I applied to other schools, too."

"And that's why you did so well at that state school, to improve your lot in life?" he asked with a raised eyebrow.

"Pretty much. I mean, I didn't think each top grade meant $1,000.00 more, or something like that, but yes," I shrugged.

"That's not what I was getting at anyway.
The improvement was in your mind and in your outlook on life." He took his left index finger and tapped on his temple.

"You mean, instead of getting bogged down in Los Angeles, I left?"

"Yes," he nodded. "And you wouldn't have been able to do that if you didn't first have the *idea* of getting out. Your body followed the idea."

"Right," I agreed. "And so?" I asked curiously like a baseball player would to the hitting coach.

"Without a good work ethic, you won't get where you want to go in life. You need to take chances and be proactive."

"That makes sense. That is the West," I agreed.

"But taking chances and being proactive doesn't *ensure* your success. Sometimes it all comes down to being in the right place at the right time. And yet you have control of whether you put yourself in those right places at the right times. So luck partially comes from you. The rest of it does not, but luck is, nonetheless, a reaction to you."

"And what about faith?" I asked.

"Faith helps, too, Jack," Clayton said with an appreciative smile. "Otherwise, you never would have picked up a pen to fill out your first application for college. You wouldn't be standing next to me right now if it weren't for faith." He squeezed my shoulder softly.

"E-mail me when you can, Jack." He put his hand out to shake mine. "Definitely, Clayton," I shook his hand. We exchanged warm smiles.

At that point, Clayton entered Rockefeller. I went back to International House to get my things ready for my trip back to New York City the next day. When I sat down on the dorm bed, a cool breeze from Lake Michigan came through the window. The conversation with Clayton about the goal of my quest made me remember a session I had had with Dr. Ling. During the session, I had opened up about my brother's accident and his funeral. Recalling the session, I realized my quest was more than just growing as a result of that night in Venice beach or finding meaning in the seemingly meaningless labyrinth of the modern world.

CHAPTER 20

A Flat Bed Truck Floats In The Black Sea

"Liam was sitting in the back of the car on the right hand side. He never liked sitting in the back and he usually didn't. But he did that day, for some reason," I confided to Dr. Ling.

"Where were you the night it happened?"

"I was playing in the living room."

"And then what happened?"

"The phone rang in the kitchen. I didn't pay any attention. And then, suddenly, it started. 'Oh my God, oh my God, oh my God, oh my God, oh my God,' my mother started shrieking as she stood in the kitchen holding the phone. It was the worst sound I have ever heard in my life. It boomed throughout the house. When I ran into the kitchen, her forehead was buried in the middle of her bent arm. Her tears were all over the counter."

"Did you know what was going on?"

"No. I had no idea. I do remember my brother calling earlier in the day to get a ride home from our dad."

"'Is dad there?' I remember Liam asking me."

" 'Yea,' I said, 'but he's in the tub.'"

"'I need a ride home; can you get him?' Liam asked me."

"Did you get him?"

"No. I think I was a smart ass and told him that he would have to get a ride home. I think I was mad at him for some reason. So, no, I didn't."

"Do you wish you had?"

"To this day. My brother always defended me against the neighbors. They would always blame me for every little mischievous thing that happened to the houses in our neighborhood."

"Was he big?"

"Very imposing. He was about six feet tall, lean and muscular. He was an avid water polo player, but he had thick bones. He was built like a free safety in football."

"So you felt comfortable with him as your protector?"

"No question," I confided, "but rather than act as his shield that day, like he had done for me before, I was a fucking asshole," I said with self hatred.

"Was that the last conversation anybody from your family had with him?"

"Yes," I nodded.

"Did you understand at the time what death was about?" Ling asked.

"Not really. I thought maybe he took his motorcycle and left the country."

"But did you ever come to some resolution about it? About what death is about?" Dr. Ling asked as he looked at me seriously. I looked back uncertain of how to respond, but I did my best.

"I just thought he got lost somewhere or took a long trip," I answered. "But when I saw my mother, I started to have a glimmer of what death meant."

"What do you mean?" Ling asked.

"I would find her sitting on my sister's bed clenching my brother's picture to her chest. She would wail and rock back and forth, like the rabbis do at the Wailing Wall. As the tears streamed down her face, I would hold her in my arms and kiss her. 'It's alright, mom. Everything is going to be alright,' I would tell her, not really knowing whether everything would be alright."

"You felt, in a way, that if he had run away, she wouldn't be mourning like that."

"Right."

"Did you feel like you had become a man before your time?" Dr. Ling asked.

"I guess so. My father was always at work. The routine of it was both his escape and his prison. He never dealt with Liam's death. My sister was away at school."

"So I can see why you got along with Frank so well," Dr. Ling said. "It seems that you both grew up before your time."

I paused to think about his comment.

"The hardest thing was my mother. When I tried to comfort her, she would say, over and over again, with no consciousness, 'Where is my baby? Where is my baby? Where is my baby? Where is my baby?'"

"But did going to the funeral help you understand what happened," Dr. Ling asked. "It started to."

"Tell me about the funeral, Jack."

"The funeral was in a temple that was filled with black suits, black hats, black gloves, black shoes, black purses, black sunglasses, and a black casket. Black Cadillac sedans and a black Cadillac hearse were parked outside." I stared down at Dr. Ling's brown penny loafers and then looked back to him.

"It was a sunny day outside in Southern California, but we were in a virtual Black Sea of people inside the temple," I continued. "I remember that in this sea of black, a red carpet separated the people on the left side from those on the right side. White roses were planted throughout the temple, popping up among the attendees."

"Go on," Dr. Ling encouraged me.

"As my father, mother, sister, and I walked into the building; the red carpet drew my eyes to the black, shiny, bullet-like casket in front of us. The top part of the casket was open, like the hood of a car open to expose the engine underneath. My brother's body was there for all to see."

"What else did you see?" Ling asked.

"I looked around at my family as we walked down the red carpet towards the casket. I remember my father staring at the casket while my mother stared at my father and cried. My sister was about 20 at the time."

A loud police siren could be heard through Dr. Ling's window. I wondered whether it was going to a murder scene. New Orleans is considered to be one of the ten most dangerous cities in the Western hemisphere, along with cities in Brazil and Mexico.

"What was your dad wearing," Dr. Ling asked.

"Black tie, suit, shoes, and socks, with a crisp white shirt. His hair was cotton white and contrasted with his snake green eyes. Six feet tall, he was powerful and stocky."

"Did he cry?" Dr. Ling asked.

"No. He stood stern, as though he was standing attention to some order from his inner voice: 'Stand straight, look straight, don't say a word and, whatever you do, don't even think about having tears.'"

I paused to remember.

"He stared at my brother's lifeless body. It was like the flat bed truck that killed my brother was floating there right in front of my father's eyes."

"Boys don't cry, right, Jack?"

Dr. Ling looked into my eyes without blinking for a few seconds, I looked away towards the window, and then he continued. "Do you remember what you were thinking at the time?"

I looked back at Dr. Ling.

"I wonder why daddy is so frozen."

"And since then?"

"That his stoicism has turned him into a mummy."

Dr. Ling looked at me with soft eyes as he sipped his tea.

"It's almost like my pop gave up on life when my brother died," I concluded.

As I sat there in the I-House dorm room, I realized that part of my quest was to find something that would cure my feelings of hopelessness and fear that resulted from my brother's death. The accompanying anger was but a cousin to these feelings. I concluded from speaking with Clayton that maybe luck alone wasn't the silver bullet I had been looking for – not only to understand that decision so many moons ago in Venice, but also life's decisions in general. I knew that I needed to take some action to get lucky, just like you need to buy the lottery ticket before you can win. That action also takes faith as Clayton pointed out.

(D) FAITH

CHAPTER 21

A Long Way From Home

"Do you know where to get off for Ocean Grove?" I asked the red headed woman with freckles sitting next to me on the bus to Ocean Grove ("OG"), New Jersey. The high rises of Manhattan were in the background.

"No, but the woman in front of me does," the freckled woman said. "Who is that?" I asked.

"She goes to church with me in Brooklyn," the red head said to me with a smile. I peeked over the seat in front of me to see a burly, black lady in her mid-50s who could have been from a Norman Rockwell painting. She had graying hair, a stern face, and round reading glasses.

"Hey, Shirley," my neighbor asked over the seat, "you know what stop we have to get off at for Ocean Grove, right?"

"Yes, all good, baby. I'll let y'all know."

"She'll take care of it," the red head assured me.

"Do you live in the city?" I asked as I put my backpack underneath my seat. "Yes, in the West Village. And you?"

"I live on Mott Street."

"I love that neighborhood," she responded in an enchanting tone. "I love yours, too," looking at her with a smile.

"What is your name?" She looked at me and held out her hand. "Jack, and yours?" I asked as I shook her hand.

"Etta Parkhurst" she said.

I paused for a moment and looked toward the sprawl of Newark in the distance. I had decided to take the bus to my first summer weekend in OG. I was 33 at the time. Frank, my roommate from my days in SoHo, had invited me into his share-house with a handful of his other friends. There were a slew of different types of people on the bus: investment bankers with button down collars, anarchy punks who hadn't taken a shower in a while, surfer dudes with blond hair down to their shoulders, and some Jersey shore muscle guys who had trimmed eyebrows and shaved bodies.

"Where are you from, Etta?"

"Montana," she said with a smile. "But my family is originally from Vandalia, Illinois, way back when. One of my ancestors, Charley, was a big time nightclub owner in the state. She was a real frontier woman who ran around with an alleged outlaw named Blue." That explained her earthy but certainly gothic style. She was wearing a black peasant dress that went down to her knees, brown hemp Mary Jane shoes, and a faded bohemian but chic black purse by Hobo. Her thick brown hair hung to her waist and was tied in a ponytail that rested ever so naturally on her back.

"Wow. You are a long way from home!" I said with surprise. "I haven't met many people from that state."

"Yes, indeed," she started to pull out her *New York Times* to read. She briefly looked it over, put it down on her lap, and then turned to me:

"And you, Jack? Where are you from?"

"Los Angeles," I turned over to her, away from the book I was reading, *Stumbling Upon Happiness.*

"You, too, are a long way from home," she said with a grin. "Yes, yes, I am," I smiled.

And then there was a pause. She broke the silence:

"Do you have children, Jack?" She slightly turned her body so as to angle it more towards me.

"No, and you?"

"Yes," she nodded, "I have a 23 year old who lives in Portland, Oregon."

"Wow! You look great. I never would have thought that you were old enough to have a 23 year old."

"Thanks," she showed me a coy smile.

"Do you go to church a lot, I mean, that is how you know the lady in front, right?" I put a bookmark in my book and closed it.

"Yes, quite a bit," she nodded.

I looked up towards the slightly peeling roof of the bus, and then looked back towards Etta:

"I remember a phrase in Spanish from Gabriel Marquez, the one who wrote *One Hundred Years of Solitude*. Have you ever read that book?

"No."

"Excellent stuff. Anyway, the phrase went something like this, and I might butcher it, but here it goes: 'El principio de la sabiduria es el temor de Dios.'"

"What does it mean?" Etta asked.

"It translates into something like, 'The beginning of wisdom is the fear of God.'"

When I said this, I looked down toward my sandals and thought back to Venice Beach. I wondered whether I had a fear of God that night. I wondered whether I have ever been wise.

"Do you remember that because you are religious?" she asked. I looked up:

"Not really. I guess I would say I am more spiritual. And you?"

"I go to a church next to my apartment in Brooklyn every Sunday." She paused and crossed her legs.

"I was kind of brought up on it in Montana. I guess the church enables me to meet nice people. It's a good way to build a community."

She paused again and looked out the window:

"I believe God is everywhere. But God is particularly present in church," she looked back at me with her deep brown eyes.

"Tickets, please," a sturdy Chinese man came along the aisle asking for tickets. Etta and I handed our tickets to the man.

As we did, I heard a Jersey girl behind us talking:

"I told haw, I told haw, that bitch better stay away from him dis summa, or else dere going to be some problems down at that beach. Franky going to have some serious fucking problems."

Etta turned to me and smirked:

"Sounds like she might be a good partner for you, eh, Jack?"

I turned around to peek and saw a big breasted, Italian-looking woman with long pink fingernails that had rings in them, a tight "Pink" tank top,, and cut-off jeans. Her hair was big and filled with Hair Net, the spray that keeps your hair in place even when you sleep on it. My grandmother used to put it on her red hair to make it look like a helmet during the day.

I smiled at the Jersey queen. She smiled back at me and then kept talking. Then Etta asked me:

"So can I ask you something Jack?" I turned to her.

"Sure."

"When you say that you are spiritual, what do you mean?" She asked with a raised eyebrow. "Being from California, do you have a little Buddha statute with candles all around it in your bedroom? Or, um, do you eat organic everything and think that brings you closer to God?"

"No Buddha, but I do have a picture of David Haselhoff from *Baywatch*, the television show, that I pray to every morning. That's spiritual, no?"

We smiled at each other.

"But, seriously, that's a tough question. Let me see if I can answer it." I looked outside, and then looked back at her:

"I guess the best way I can answer is like this. I remember the question I had to answer in order to get into college. It went something like this – how did the Copernican revolution and Darwin's theory of evolution undermine self-love?"

"And?" Etta asked.

"Well, Copernicus was the one who said we were not the middle of the universe, but that the sun was."

"Ok, and?"

"And Darwin was the one who said we basically evolved from apes."

"Ok, so?"

"The answer I gave was that both men were revolutionary because they basically took away our sense of self-importance."

"Meaning what?"

"We are not special. We are not creations made in the image of God no more than the ape is a special creation made to mirror God."

I looked down for a second to evade her look, and then looked back up toward her.

"So," Etta said with a curious tone, "people inferred from Darwin and Copernicus that there was no God?"

"I think some did. And what do you think?" I asked her.

"It seems that you have to start with the darkness," Etta said with a deadpan face.

"You mean like when you put your head under the bed covers?" I smirked. "What do you mean?"

CHAPTER 22

"Started Counting My Blessings"

Etta looked straight ahead, like she was getting ready for an appearance on stage, and then back towards me.

"What I mean is that faith is really a leap that you take," she made a motion with her hand over the seat in front of her. "It is kind of like moving to live somewhere you have never been before."

She paused.

"Ever had to do that, Jack?"

"Yes," I nodded. "I moved to Chicago from Los Angeles without ever having set one foot in the city."

"Well then," she nodded, "when you were about to move to Chicago, you thought you could make it there, but you didn't know for sure?"

"I thought I could, but I wasn't sure, no," I shrugged.

"Precisely," she pointed at me with her right index finger, "and that is where faith comes into play. You take a leap believing you can make it in Chicago, or wherever it is you move to . . . but you don't know for sure until you actually do the move."

"But you can tell – you can gauge whether you are going to be able to make it in the new city because you have succeeded at other new things before," I said in retort.

"What about a city outside the United States? What about a country you haven't been to before, like Denmark?" Etta asked.

I paused to think about what she had told me. She continued:

"All I am trying to say is that faith isn't like math. In math, one thing automatically follows from another," she put her index finger, middle finger, and ring finger up, "one plus one equals two, and so on." She had long, pale hands and fingers, elegant and Victorian looking.

"So how is faith different? I go to confession, talk about my sins, and then, presto, I am forgiven! Isn't that how it goes down?" I asked with a mischievous grin.

"Things don't follow so easily," Etta shook her head slightly. "When you open your eyes to see the sun light in the morning, it is only through the grace of God."

"So we are living for a purpose, you think?" I asked.

"Yes," she nodded. "I believe you are alive for a reason," Etta said with a smile.

I sat silent. This was a new thought to me. So I looked outside. I remembered back to Frank's "sex, money, and murder" tattoo, and to my conversation with Dr. Ling about how the only thing many people seem to respect is violence. I turned to Etta:

"What about all of the bad stuff that happens in the world?" I looked at her with a serious look. "How do you explain all of this bad stuff happening and there being a God?"

"There is no explaining it. But there is a way to use that bad stuff. Instead of constantly living your life in fear of it, practice being grateful for the times you have away from it. That's what I have been trying to do, Jack."

She paused.

"And I have seen it the worst of it. My parents were church going people, but my father was an abusive drunk," she said cryptically as she looked outside the bus window.

"What do you mean?" I kept looking at her.

Etta turned her deep dark brown eyes on me. They conveyed the full message. I turned to stare towards the back of the seat in front of me, briefly closed my eyes, looked down towards my shoes, and imagined what happened.

I opened my eyes to look back towards Etta. She was staring straight towards the front of the bus, toward the road, toward a path that has brought her farther and farther away from home. And yet that is precisely where she wants to be. I looked away from her and to the sprawling Jersey shore landscape outside. We drove by rows and rows of beautiful mansions.

"Did your mother know?" I asked. "No," she looked away.

She hesitated.

"I felt it was my fault at the time," she said as though she were speaking to the dirty bus window. "I haven't told many people about it. I have tried to kind of hide it, and my feelings from it, all of these years."

She hesitated again.

"It happens more than you would think, and it often happens in the families where you would least expect it." She looked back at me.

"Smooth waters run deep," I said to her. "Is it generational?"

"I think it is," she nodded.

"And your mom didn't say anything?"

"No. Even if she knew, and I'm sure she did, she didn't want to lose the family."

"It's like the uncertainty of leaving was worse than the actuality of her situation?"

"Maybe," Etta shrugged. "Regardless, that is why I left Montana. I wanted to get far away from all of that."

She paused. And then:

"The universe has messages for us, Jack."

"But isn't seeing those messages kind of like being crazy? Isn't it like seeing something that isn't there?" I asked.

"It's not. Crazy is doing the same thing over and over again and expecting a different outcome. Faith enables you to do things in your life that those without faith are unable to do."

I looked at her skeptically but also with an open mind. I thought to myself: if this woman can still have faith after all that she has been through, then why shouldn't I be able to have the same faith?

She interrupted my thoughts:

"You are from Los Angeles, right?"

"Yup."

"Did you know that many artists give God credit for their fame?"

"Most of them are made to look like Devil worshippers," I chuckled.

"Yes, they are thought of as being Devil worshippers. But look at Willie Nelson, the country western singer. My son loves him. I read about him in an interview with someone, where Willie said something like 'when I started counting my blessings, my while life turned around.'"

"Then there is luck, too, Etta," I said. "Some people aren't exactly religious or spiritual – and yet they might be awfully lucky. I met a man in Chicago, a prominent journalist, who survived World War II and three wives. When I asked him how he did it, he gave me no secret recipe, no prophecy. He merely turned to me and said something like, 'luck, and, oh yea, I didn't smoke.'"

"Technically, I know what you are saying, Jack, but I still think God had a purpose for him, too," Etta insisted.

"Regardless, I guess I kind of believe that people have an energy that is there for you to tap into, just like the photographer in Chicago was there for me to tap into. But, whether you call it luck or faith, physics says we are all made of particles and that these particles rub together to make a certain energy happen."

"Like atoms running into one another," Etta observed. "Or better yet bumper cars hitting one another?" she said with a smirk.

"You could say that . . . I guess what I am trying to say is that negative thinking has the effect of making negative things happen to your body, and to the world around you."

"Meaning?" Etta said with a contorted face.

CHAPTER 23

Security Blankets Can Stifle

As we got closer to Asbury Park, I nervously shook my leg for a few seconds, looked outside the bus toward some of the surfers taking waves into the ocean, and then looked back towards Etta:

"I think the best example I can give is of a cousin of mine in Los Angeles."

"What's his name?"

"Frank."

"And what about Frank makes you think of him?"

The Jersey girl behind us was smacking her gum loudly and blowing big bubbles. I looked back at her, and she was twirling her hair.

"Because Frank is angry," I answered Etta as I turned around. "And I understand why," I said.

"Why?"

"His father left him when he was younger. Pretty much abandoned him and his mother. And so Frank took another path when he got older – started dealing in high school, dropped out, got into the trade heavily, began rolling with gangs from L.A., got sleeved up,"

"Sleeved up?"

"Tattoos on his arms. His arms are full of tattoos."

"I get it."

"I have always loved Frank. He is kind of an older brother to me. He protects me." I nodded and looked out the bus window.

"But I wonder if Frank's anger keeps him from the very thing he missed when he was younger – a family of his own," I shrugged.

"Keeps him from being a father, and a good one at that?" She looked at me softly.

"I am sure he would be, but I think he may be so wedded to his anger that he wouldn't know what to do without it."

"It's kind of like his security blanket," Etta pointed out. "Don't leave home without it."

"In a way. I just wonder if he was ever able to take that leap, that jump, into the future without losing that security blanket."

The Jersey girl was talking on the phone again, this time to Franky, her lover:

"Yo, Franky, what you doin with that skank? A little birdy told me you hookin up wid hah," she said smacking her gum, "I better not find out dis shit is true . . . or else you going to be in big fucking trouble," she said interrupting herself to blow more bubbles.

"I wouldn't want to be Franky right now," Etta said with a grin. "So, going back to Frank, it seems like you have been struggling with, um, the same feelings?" Etta asked.

"In a way," I confided in her.

"I see," Etta said on the heels of my comment. "I think that it's hard to have faith if all you do is act out of anger. It is easy to be angry. It is easy to be destructive. The real challenge is love. So perhaps God put Frank in your path to show you that you have a choice as to how you live your life?"

I pondered her comment.

"I also think that God puts other people in your path for small minutes of salvation like when you are down or depressed," she continued.

"What do you mean?" I asked.

"I'll give you an example," she said as she looked back towards me.

I was expecting her to tell me about some encounter with a priest. But then she surprised me.

CHAPTER 24

Luigi's Pizza Joint

After the bus hit a bump in the road that brought Etta and me slightly off our seats, she looked over at me:

"New York can be a lonely place for someone who is not from around here – no set group of friends, family, and what have you." Etta looked down at her shoes and then looked back over at me.

"I know that all too well," I nodded in agreement.

"One night, I was feeling particularly lonely. It was during the winter when the streets are vacant, the sky is overcast, and the air is frigid."

She paused to gather her thoughts.

"I felt like there was nobody around to talk to about things. I felt like I could not count on the people I thought I could count on."

She paused again. I didn't say anything. "It was disorienting."

She paused.

"I didn't tell you this, but I am divorced." I looked at her sadly.

"I thought so highly of my husband," she smiled as she looked out the window remembering the good times with him. "We got married kind of young and so I guess I didn't see the real him," she looked back at me. "I was so fixated on getting married that I didn't think about what would happen after I got married."

I kept quiet as she opened up.

"Let's just say that it did not work out." She briefly looked down as though she were ashamed. She looked back up to me: "I found out that he was not the person I thought I loved. My parents were so excited when I married him. But he was a heavy drinker. I think they had premonitions, but I don't think they cared."

"That's odd. I remember two California kids telling me a story like that in Amsterdam," I thought to myself reflecting back to Andy and Kelly.

"I guess it's a small world, eh, Jack?" she said with a small smile. "Totally," I looked at her with a surprised look.

"It seems it is like those types of encounters, like the one you had with the California kids, that can sometimes shed light on things."

She paused.

"Or another example is some people that I met in this Brooklyn pizza parlor."

"I love Brooklyn pizza joints," I smiled.

She looked towards the front of the bus to gather her thoughts.

As she did, I heard the Jersey girl behind us get another call. Her phone rang the song "Walk Like a Man, Talk Like Man." She picked up the phone and answered: "Yea, yea, yea, I'll be there the whole weekend, Jimmy, what you guys doin' tomorraw night?" The Jersey girl paused. "Stone Pony? Awesome. I'll meet you guys at 8, dat's when de show stawts, right? OK." The Jersey girl smacked her gum when she spoke, and blew some bubbles, too, like it was her theme music. I looked back at her with intrigue. She smiled and waved at me. I smiled and then looked back at Etta.

"The parlor was called Luigi's. It is in the middle of the Midwood section of Brooklyn, not far from Sheepshead Bay and Brighton Beach," Etta explained.

"What's it like?"

"It is a puny place with pictures of Italians on the walls, like Joe Dimaggio, Robert De Niro, and others. The parlor smelled of fresh garlic, tomato, cheese, and baking bread. There was this old looking brick oven in the back."

I thought back to the brick ovens I had seen in Naples.

"So I walked in to get a slice and went to sit down," she continued. "Sitting across the way from the spot I wanted to sit," she motioned with her hand, "was this black lady who was wearing an MTA shirt and hat."

"MTA?" I asked.

"Metropolitan Transit Authority."

"Oh."

"I asked her if I could sit in the seat across from her. She said 'yes' in a soft tone. She was about 60 and had dark black, dry skin. Her slice of pizza was next to her."

"'Going or coming?' I asked as I sat down."

"'Coming, I just got off my shift. 12 hours,' the MTA woman answered."

"'Wow,' I said in surprise."

"'Especially sitting in a booth. I can't really leave it. Except to go to the bathroom, or for something like that,' the MTA woman said to me."

"'Where are you from?' I asked her."

"'West Virginia,' she told me in a very quiet, sweet voice."

"'You are a long way from home,' I said to her."

I interjected:

"Kind of like you and me, huh, Etta?"

Etta smiled and continued:

"'Yup,' she said to me."

"'Do you still have family down there?' I asked."

"Yes,' she answered. 'But all I want to do right now is to get into my bed and sleep. My next shift is at 9,' she told me."

"'Tomorrow night, I hope,' I said."

"'Yes,' she answered."

"'Do you like pizza?' I asked."

"'Yes, it's this place and Carmine's that I like,' she answered." Etta interrupted her story and said to me:

"Jack, I couldn't help myself from thinking how cute this woman was. She was so matter of fact. She just got off this shift, and she wasn't complaining about things. She was just enjoying her pizza. A very simple pleasure."

"I get it," I said to Etta.

"I then asked the MTA lady, 'Where is Carmine's?'"

"'Off the L train,' she answered."

"'You mean in Brooklyn?'"

"'Yup,' she nodded her head, 'It's not far from the Lorimer stop.'"

"'So you only go there and here?' I asked."

"'Yup. These are the only two,' she answered."

"She finished her pizza and I wished her a good night," Etta explained to me. "Her demeanor comforted me. Her calm. Her stoicism."

I looked at Etta in appreciation of the story she just told me, and then commented as the warm Jersey sun came in through the windows:

"There are so many people in this city that have so much more than she, and yet they always seem unhappy," I observed. "Perhaps it's easy to lose sight of simple things when you are so fixated on the complex."

I paused as I heard the rumbling of the Academy bus in the background. I then asked Etta:

"So who was the owner of this pizza place anyway?"

"Luigi Bonaparte."

She smiled to herself.

"He was one of the most colorful – or the most colorful – Brooklyn – or should I say Queens? – Italian-Americans I have ever met. The guy had the thickest accent – he 'twacks lik dat,'" Etta said to me.

"I know these types well," I said. I thought back to my grandmother's thick Brooklyn accent. When she said "water" she pronounced it "watah."

"I remember Luigi explaining to me, after I told him I wanted to meet some real New York guys, something like: 'You wanna meet a real New Yowka? Go out in Bay Ridge, sister. Yeh, you'll find yourself some real New Yawkas dea.'"

"What did he look like?" I asked with one raised eyebrow.

"Rotund. He had a pot belly," Etta made a big circular motion over her belly. "The blob softly balanced between staying inside his shirt and pants and making its escape to the outside world. I remember his hands were thick and calloused. He used to waddle with his arms out to the sides because his stockiness stopped him from walking with them close to his side."

"Like an Italian penguin!" I said.

"He had tattoos on each forearm. One was a pin-up type woman with an anchor, whereas the other was a flower wrapped around a long knife. His hair was black and slicked back and his eyes, too, were olive black. He stood about five foot six. He told me he was from Sicily."

I heard Etta's friend in front of us opening up a crinkly bag of potato Claytons. She turned over in her seat and asked us:

"Y'all want some Claytons."

"No thank you," Etta answered. "Jack?"

"No thanks," I answered.

"Very well, more for me," the woman said playfully and turned back around in her seat.

I looked back over to Etta.

"And what did Luigi say about New York men?" I asked. "He spoke more about the women in New York, surprisingly."

"I'd love to hear about this."

"I remember him telling me about the 'gold diggers' from Manhattan. I'll try and impersonate as best as I can: 'I sayz to ha, you wanna tak ma Eskowt, ga ahed,' and when he said 'Eskowt' he meant the Ford Escort. 'There ain't no gold in deh, doh, baby.'"

I smiled at this all natural looking prairie woman speaking with a pretty damn good Brooklyn accent.

"'Yea sister,' Luigi told me, 'you get yerself to Bay Ridge. You meet yourself a real good New Yawka there.'"

"'What about you, Luigi?' I asked him. 'Where do you go to meet women?'" As Etta said this to me, she adjusted herself in her seat so as to see me better.

"And? What was Luigi's thought on that one?" I asked Etta. "This is what I remember him telling me."

She paused so she could get into character.

"'Well, ya see, sister, themz galz in Manhattan get lost in their heads. Yea, they got a good job. Yea, they dress real nice, ya know, but, dem gals ain't men.'"

"I love the accent, Etta. Bravo!" I smiled.

"I'm trying here, Jack." She got back into character.

"And so he continued: 'I mean, ya see sister, one of them gals can touch a little one like dis,' and then he grabbed my arm softly, 'but they can't go grabbin the little one like dis,' at which point Luigi grabbed my arm more forcefully."

"You must have loved speaking to this guy. What a character!"

"I did!" Etta grinned. "So let me see if I can finish his spiel to me. So he says to me: 'My point is, sister, I'm all for them gals makin' it, and all dat, you know, but, eh, they ain't men. I tink dat dey get all whacked in their heads in Manhattan being in dem offices and what not all day. Dat ain't de real world, sister. Dis is de real world,' as Luigi pointed his index and middle finger at his eyes, staring at me."

"Intense guy," I observed.

"Yes," Etta responded. "But he was a real pepperoni philosopher. He wasn't the most polished guy. But he had a lot of very insightful things to say."

"Entertaining at the very least. And, yes, thought provoking, especially for a random pizza place," I said to Etta. I thought of Frank when I said this. Like Luigi, Frank was not polished. But, like Luigi, Frank had a lot of insightful things to say. I guess that is one of the reasons part of me wanted to be like him.

"I especially remember what he said to me about the economy," Etta said. "What's that?"

Again I heard the Jersey girl behind us smacking her gum and blowing big bubbles.

"I remember him saying something like this about it all: 'Yea, sister, people bitch and moan about the economy. It was like dis in the 80s. I bawght dis place from a family friend. I come here every day from Queens. I been here 12 years. Tru tik and tin, ya know. I look back on it now – and laugh.'"

"'Why?' I asked him," Etta said to me. "And then Luigi gave me his answer: 'Because I realized: as long I have my health and faith,' I have everything, sister,' he told me with a crooked Brooklyn smile."

"He then said something to me, Jack, which makes me remember him, and my MTA dining friend from West Virginia, to this day: 'You'll look back on this time in a few years and laugh, too, sister.'"

"When I left the pizza parlor that night after spending about an hour there, Luigi gave me a warm hug. It was so nice to feel that affection and safety from someone who was a complete stranger," Etta reminisced.

I paused when Etta said this, closed my eyes, and reflected for a moment. I opened my eyes and then said:

"So how was this kind of like your church in Brooklyn? I mean, do you think it shows that God is everywhere, like you were saying before?" I asked.

I wanted to hear how she used her faith as a caretaker for her pain. I hoped to learn how I could use faith as a salve, too.

CHAPTER 25

A Brooklyn Church

"Well, when I get lonely, or even when I have ideas of getting revenge back in Montana, who do you think I think of to give me comfort?" Etta asked.

"Richard Simmons, the trainer?" I said in jest. She smiled.

"Close! I think of God," she looked at me with her dark brown eyes, "and God is in people like Luigi and the stoic MTA lady. In them, I find inspiration, not desperation. They made me so warm and welcome that night. It was as if God were reaching out and saying, 'Look, these are people you can reach out to, so do it. If they can do it, you can, too.'"

"So I guess what you are saying is that New York City has soul, you just have to look out for it? " I asked Etta.

"I think so."

She paused to think.

"But I have found that you will not necessarily find faith in the bowels of a church. Sometimes you will find it in the person sitting right next to you on the subway, at the pizza parlor, or wherever you may find other New Yorkers." Etta broke a small smile.

As she did, we both heard the Jersey girl in the back of us: "Yea, girls. We goin' to have some fun tonight, eh! De bus is amost deah. I see you girlz in about 15, awright?" Of course, she smacked her gum and blew some bubbles.

Etta and I smiled at the sound of the Jersey lass. I continued our chat:

"But you aren't going to have these types of experiences with everyone in New York City," I pointed out.

"Of course not. That's why that night was so special. There are a lot of people in this city who care only about keeping up with the Joneses. They'll help you only if it gets them to where they want to go."

I paused to think of what she said.

"I can see that," I agreed. "Sometimes your friends or acquaintances will need you. Helping them won't make you money. And I guess that's why many are not inclined to help one another unless there is something 'in it for them.'"

"That's what that night in the Brooklyn pizza parlor told me about this city," Etta said. "There is spirit here, there is soul here, and people have faith here. It is just a matter of tapping into the right pools of people," she said to me with a warm smile.

At this point, the bus arrived at Etta's stop close to Ocean Grove. She got up, gathered her things, and then turned to me:

"Always remember that God is there when you close your eyes, regardless if you are in the church, on the street, or wherever you are. It was a pleasure meeting you, Jack." She looked at me with far away eyes.

"And you, too, Etta."

We gave each other a solid hug.

(E) COURAGE

CHAPTER 26

What Were The Dots?

"When the first plane hit the World Trade Center, it sounded like a sonic boom," I said to Christine Beem, an alternative looking 33-year-old preppy stunner. She stood about five foot nine and had freckled Irish skin. After I got onto the number 6 subway train at the 86th Street stop heading downtown one cool afternoon, I thought about Christine. Like me, she had just moved back to New York. Unlike me, she lost her father on September 11. I met her when I was 31.

While her bone structure was model thin, she had a strong presence. She wore tortoise colored retro cat framed glasses, a white Gap blouse, an orange scarf, grey J. Crew slacks with cuffs, brown penny loafers, and green and white argyle socks. She had clear nail polish, and wore a silver Tag Heuer diving watch along with silver bracelets. On her left ring finger she wore what looked like a silver graduation ring from college. Her graying black Irish brown hair hung in a long pony tail that went to the middle of her back.

"Did you see any of it?" Christine asked with her pale Irish looking lips – dark and somewhat freckled – as she looked at me with her large, button-like brown eyes.

"I heard the first one hit, but I saw the second plane hit. I was getting ready to go to the office, and then, all of a sudden, I heard the boom." I smacked my hands together. And then I noticed that Christine's nose was flat like a boxer's, and seemed like it was swollen.

"Where were you living?" Christine asked. "On Broome Street in SoHo."

"So that was the first one?" she asked.

"Yep. But I didn't have any windows in the loft. We lived on the top floor of the building, and we had only skylights. So I didn't think anything of it until I heard the screaming and crying."

"Screaming and crying?"

"My neighbor and her cute little daughter, Georgia, were standing outside my door screaming and crying. So when I heard them I knew something was wrong. I opened the door and they pointed through the small window on the floor to the hole in the first tower."

"What did you think?"

"I thought it was some guy who got drunk and flew his plane through the building. We went up to the roof to watch the smoke come out of the tower. As we did, we saw the second plane approach."

"And what did you guys think then?"

"That it was a fire plane to put out the flames. But then we saw it smash into the second tower, causing a gush of flames to come out, with glass going everywhere. Little dots of things starting coming out of the towers heading towards the ground."

"What were the dots?"

"People," I said to Christine grimly.

As the number six train stopped at the 77th Street stop, I remembered that, around 6:00 p.m. the night I had met Christine, I had come to her Brooklyn Heights apartment to see about subletting a room in her apartment. I knocked on her long, black, gothic door.

"And you are Jack?" She smiled and held out her hand after she opened the door. We had spoken on the phone earlier that week so she was expecting me.

"And you are Christine." I smiled back and shook her hand. "Nice to meet you."

"Nice to meet you, too," I answered.

As I entered her apartment, we walked down a long and narrow entry hall. It had a frayed Persian rug on the old wood floor. There was a large vintage painting of witches and nuns eating lunch at a long table in what looked like a church courtyard. It looked like some were spitting red wine at each other from their glasses, while others sat, drank, and cracked up. An eye-patched priest sat among them, covering his eyes, but you could make out a little rascal smile. I stood and stared at the photo wondering what they were laughing at.

Christine looked over at me:

"Oh, yeah, that. One of my ancestors, Emerald, lived in San Francisco and gave refuge to an alleged witch from Salem during the 1800s. This painting has been passed down in my family since then. I think it was given to her by the supposed witch."

"Is that wine?" I asked. She shrugged.

"Nah," she smiled mischievously at me. "It's their bloody Mary mix." I stared at her.

"Let's go into the living room," she said as she walked.

We took a left into the living room with its 15-foot high ceilings, panoramic size mirrors, and paintings of revolutionary figures hanging on the walls. Because the brownstone was built sometime in the 1800s, it had a colonial energy to it. The springs in her red velvet couch screeched when we sat down.

"Do you want something to drink?" Christine asked. "How about a glass of red wine? I have some Malbec from Argentina."

"That would be great, thank you," I nodded.

Christine got up off the couch and went into the kitchen. She came back with a bottle of wine and two glasses. After she poured the wine, I took one glass, and she took the other.

"Cheers," she said.

"Cheers."

We took big sips.

"So where are you staying right now?" she asked. "Carroll Gardens," I answered.

Carroll Gardens, Brooklyn, is about a 10 to 15 minute walk to Christine's apartment in Brooklyn Heights.

"Lived there long?"

"Actually, no. I am just staying with the sister of a good friend of mine from New Orleans. I just moved back from there."

She sipped her wine.

"I've never been there. I have heard amazing things about it. How long did you live there?"

"Five years."

"So how did you end up in New York?" I sipped my wine.

"I moved here with my girlfriend."

"From New Orleans?"

"Yea."

"Did you live with her in New Orleans?"

"Yea."

"Are you guys still together? I mean do you plan on staying with her here?"

"No."

Christine looked at me curiously. So I offered up the explanation after taking another sip of wine.

"She moved back to France about two weeks after we moved into our apartment here.

And then, about a year after September 11, I decided to move back to New Orleans."

"Why?"

I remember wondering why Christine was so curious about me. I later understood after learning more about her loss, and the fact that she never really left the northeast. I gathered she was in a sort of fish bowl.

"Well, to be honest with you, to retreat," I answered.

She looked up to the engraved ceiling of the apartment, as if reflecting on herself or history, and then looked back to me.

"How long did you live in New Orleans this time around?" she asked. "I lived there for about two years."

"So you met some good people down there? You liked it?" I took a sip of my wine.

"Yes. I loved it," I nodded with a mischievous smile. "Why?"

"My life there was so different than the way I was living in New York. I also met some amazing people down there who gave me the courage to come back here."

She looked at me reflectively. "They are opposites. Although, come to think of it, New York used to be more like New Orleans. But now I think the more ambitious, smart, and powerful come here."

"Generally, I think you are right," I agreed. "But there are some who appear to be powerless who are actually very powerful down there."

She took a big sip of her wine. "Like?"

I thought about whether I should share with her about Alby and the others I met down in New Orleans. Christine was warm so I felt like I could. I also felt like she needed some companionship. I did, too.

I answered:

"A retired pilot who could fly upside down in a propeller plane for hours. Now he's a doctor."

Christine looked at me surprised and with raised eyebrows. She took a big gulp of her wine after she poured a splash into her glass.

"What's his name?" she asked with intrigue.

CHAPTER 27

Alby, Et Al.

"Alby. That's whose sister I am staying with in Carroll Gardens." She got more comfortable on the old couch.

"Who is he? I mean what's his story?"

"Alby O'Brien is about 67 year old and is from an old-line Irish family in New Orleans. They did a lot of contracts for the federal government – munitions, construction, among other things."

"Is Alby his real name?" she asked with a raised eyebrow.

"Yup, full name is Dr. Alby O'Brien."

"How did you meet him?"

"I met him one day in front of an organic market on Magazine Street in New Orleans." I took a healthy sip of my wine.

"And what was Alby like? I mean is he a big guy?"

I could tell Christine liked the story I was telling her about Alby. It was somehow taking her away from a melancholy that seemed a part of her.

"No, not at all," I looked around her apartment to think of how to describe Alby, and then went on with it: "He is about five foot ten, tall cowboy build, rich gray-brown Irish hair, big sandy light brown eyes. He dresses real simple – shorts or jeans, t-shirt, sandals. Alby drives a vintage black convertible Ferrari with brown interior sometimes. At others, he rides a distressed looking green Linus bike with 'bruised ego' written with white paint on the side."

"A real character. It sounds like he was down and out?"

"That is his act. It is a self-defense mechanism."

"Against what?"

"Initially," I said.

"Sounds like me after September eleventh," she admitted quickly as if she didn't want to talk too much about it. She sipped her wine for a moment and then just sat there.

As a number of Hunter College students came onto the subway at the 68th Street/Hunter College stop, I thought back to how I felt like Christine and I had a lot in common. But I couldn't put my finger on it during the first part of the evening with her.

"Why do you say that?" she asked. "I mean about him running from initially.."

"Because he was divorced four times, twice from the same woman. I remember him telling me how he married a real young girl who was like 20 years younger than he was and, after finishing their list of sexual exploits, they got divorced!" I smirked.

"I wonder how many exploits he had on that list?"

"I think he told me once, like 40 or something!" I smirked again. "But I think the woman he married twice broke his heart. That's the one who touched him, as I understand things. After their second divorce, he smoked a lot of grass, drank a lot of booze, got rid of his furniture, and lived a very Spartan life. But, by acting crazy and down and out, he was able to keep the faint hearted at bay. Those who saw through it as bullshit realized . . . "

I paused.

"That he had a good heart. But he was excellent at camouflaging it," I continued. "He was kind of like a good bad guy, you could say."

"And he was a doctor all the while doing all of this?"

"Yup, worked at Charity Hospital, in the emergency room. I think that's why he did all of the smoking and such, to get away from all of the demons that he had in his head from all of those bodies he would see coming in."

"I would probably be doing the same thing if I were him. You know I'm good at camouflaging my emotions, too," she said. "So I can relate to that."

"Down below, beyond the cynical act, he is a good man, having produced movies, with his own money, like *Left Behind*, the untold story New Orleans public schools. He is very giving. I mean, the last time I went down to New Orleans with a friend, we went to dinner with Alby at Crescent City Steaks. There was no check at the end of the meal. Alby took care of the check before it came. And, over dinner, or when we would hang out, Alby would often say to me, 'do as I say, *not* as I do.' He reminded me of my cousin back in L.A. He would say the same thing to me."

"Was that Alby's way of mentoring you?"

"I guess you could say that. I mean, instead of saying to me, 'do as I say, and as I do,' or 'as I have done,' he was realistic about himself. I think he knew his shortcomings. It's like his . . . "

"Head said one thing, but his body did another?" Christine interrupted.

"That sounds about right. He also used to tell me not to worry about where I would be in five years. He would say: 'Jack, if we knew what was going to happen in the next five years in life, wouldn't it all be so very boring? Part of the excitement of life *is* the anarchy!' And boy did he get into it!"

"How so?" she asked.

"I remember him telling me how he fell in love with this stripper who was a heroin addict and who ended up in the Louisiana State Penitentiary. He used to tell me how he knew she wasn't right for him, but he loved their sex and other escapades. Alby was a sharp guy. He was nobody's fool. But his desires often got the better of him, made him do really stupid things that were disrespectful to his own intelligence."

"As they do with many of us," Christine chimed in. "Look at how many people out there are addicts to bad relationships, drugs, booze, food, money, and the list goes on and on. The thing is, I am sure if you asked many of these folks whether they thought what they were doing was good for them, they would tell you that they knew it wasn't," Christine said.

"And yet they continue doing it anyway," I said as I sipped my wine.

"That's why there are all of these wellness centers in the marketplace. I read about one in Malibu called Passages. It charges $88,500 per treatment, or something like that," she pointed out.

"In an odd way, Alby was like a wellness center for me."

"I could sense that," Christine said. "So he kind of played the part of a disappointed angel?"

"Or fallen. My cousin in Los Angeles was the same way. He would always give me great advice, but wouldn't take it himself."

"At least Alby said it, I mean vocalized it."

"Totally."

"And you guys used to talk about this stuff over meals together?"

"Usually at the Crescent City Steakhouse."

"So he did have money? His pauper thing was an act?"

"In a way, no, in a way, yes."

"Why do you say no?"

"Because Alby actually lived the life."

"What do you mean?" she asked curiously.

"Well, for one thing, his house is in the Lower Ninth Ward."

"Which is where?"

"It's the largest and most eastward ward in New Orleans."

"A ward?"

"Ah, yes, New Orleans is split into 17 voting wards. Think of each of the ward as a voting district in the city."

"Are the Lower and Upper Ninth Wards different not only in name?"

"Totally," I nodded. "The Upper Ninth has the Bywater and other neighborhoods that are full of racially mixed hipsters, writers, dealers, bartenders, doctors, and a slew of other people. The Lower Ninth, unlike the Upper Ninth, is all black, save for a few white folks like Alby. Fats Domino has lived in the Lower Ninth for years and not far from Alby. The Upper Ninth is also located up the river from the lower, which is closer to St. Bernard Parish."

"So where exactly does Alby live?"

"He lives in a ratty old house a few blocks from the river. He bought the place for like $25,000. Most of the homes on the street were either falling apart, or have already fallen apart. Across from his house was a place called the Cadillac Lounge."

"The Lower Ninth is the one that got hit hardest by Katrina, if I remember correctly."

"It was. Totally underwater."

"So who hangs out at this Lounge then?"

"Locals. I think a lot of them had been patients of his at Charity, and so many were still living because of his medical skills."

"How do you know?"

"I went there with Alby one time, and they welcomed him in like he was part of the family there."

She took a big gulp of her wine. "What was that like?"

"It was welcoming."

"Welcoming?" she said with surprise.

"Yes, welcoming. I remember there was a sign next to the mirror that said 'come in as a stranger, leave as a friend.' Another sign said 'attitude is everything.' The whole place was mostly full of grey haired folks around 50 or so. The place from the outside was very broken down, and the same was physically true about the inside."

"How so?" She sipped more wine.

"There was peeling white paint on the outside of the bar. There was also a water line from where the flooding had reached when Katrina had hit. The inside also had peeling white paint and peeling wood floors."

She looked at me as we both took another sip of our wine. And then I thought out loud: "And yet the fact that the place was falling apart didn't seem to affect the people's attitudes."

"How could it not matter?" she asked.

"It didn't seem like it did. When I came inside with Alby, people were smiling away and listening to Louie Armstrong's 'La Vie En Rose.'"

"I love that song," Christine said.

"Me, too. So, when Alby and I went to the bar to have some Budweiser bottles, the owner kissed Alby on each cheek."

"What was the owner's name?"

"Her name was Mrs. Cadillac."

"I wonder if there was Mr. Cadillac?" Christine smirked.

"I bet," I said in the surfer accent that I had been brainwashed with growing up in the Valley. "She was an elegant black lady around 61 years old with graying hair and light ebony skin. She always wore a conservative-looking dress – down to the knees, covered shoulders, and high up to the neck with a long pearl necklace."

"She sounds regal," Christine said.

"She was. After Alby introduced me to her, another faster song came on – I think it was "Summertime" by Art Blakey – and some people started dancing. An older man who was dancing behind us yelled and waved for me to come dance with one of the women on the floor. And so I did! Alby and I spent the afternoon there. It was so random!"

I paused.

"But the place was also very dangerous to outsiders, especially to those who came into the neighborhood with an attitude."

"How so?" Christine asked.

"Someone from outside the neighborhood had been murdered on the street a few weeks earlier."

"I wouldn't have gone near that place," Christine shook her head.

"I wouldn't have if I hadn't known Alby. He told me about how this guy came in from one of the other neighborhoods in the Ninth Ward. But, from what Alby told me, the family that owns the lounge is armed to the teeth with TEC – 9 and MAC – 10 submachine guns. The men pack 9-millimeter pistols. So, when this guy came into the neighborhood talking trash to the people there about how his crew was going to take over, they shot him dead."

"How did Alby know?"

"He said he was sitting inside his living room when he heard the shots. 'Dude, when I heard those shots ringing out, I hit the ground real quick,' he told me."

"There are no cops around?"

"Alby told me that cops don't come around there. They are pretty much outgunned on the block. Each house is armed, and the cops don't really want to mess around with some large- scale gun battle like that. I guess you can see that this family, and its head, played the part of a local warlord on that street in the Lower Ninth."

"And you still felt safe there? I don't think I would have had the guts to go to a place like that – even with Alby."

"Perhaps I was both stupid and brave to go there," I smirked.

"Like when you use the backs of crocodiles to get across the swamp," she retorted with a grin.

She looked at me like I was crazy.

"Oddly, yes. I did feel perfectly safe. Alby knew everyone there. He told me he introduced himself to the neighbors when he moved in. So everyone in the neighborhood knew and felt comfortable with his presence. They always said hello to him when he left the house. Plus, Alby lived in a commune with some pretty interesting folks, to say the least."

"A commune with whom?"

"There was this one guy named Tubby." Christine giggled.

"This is like learning about Frankenstein and his cousins or something," Christine said. "I mean these guys sound very macabre. Who is this Tubby?"

"A local white boy born in the Lower Ninth. His father was locked up when he was younger and so he was taken care of by his mamma. Tubby was 52 and was a grizzly 220-pound man. He had the build of Mike Ditka, the old Chicago Bears linebacker – stocky, with a barrel chest, and ape-like long, strong arms."

"Ditka -- the one with the mustache?"

"Except Tubby didn't have a mustache. He had a missing tooth in the front, and his dark Sicilian-like, black hair was balding. He had a tattoo on the right shoulder that said 'Shirley' in cursive writing."

"For his wife?"

"Got it to sleep with a girl when he was 15 and who he had his first child with when he was around 19. The schools there are so pitiful there is nothing to do other than stuff like that, it seems, or slang."

"What are the schools like?" she asked as she sipped her wine. "Pitiful shape."

"It sounds like many of the kids in the area you are talking about don't feel like they have a future."

"Totally. Nor did Tubby. He didn't ever have a true sense of hope or, if he did, he had lost it a long time ago."

"I would likely feel the same way. I think most people put in that environment would feel the same way. It would be exceptional to feel otherwise."

I nodded in agreement and sipped my wine.

"I felt the same way after September 11." She interrupted my thoughts. "It's like I was seeing an abyss," Christine confided in me as she lowered her head and closed her eyes.

I didn't want to pry. I waited until she raised her head and opened her eyes again.

"And so why did they call him 'Tubby'?" Christine said curiously after she put down her wine. "I mean I am picturing some massive man who looks like . . . "

"King Kong!" I felt like putting some levity in the talk. She looked at me with a small smile.

"Because his belly was so big," I motioned outwards like I had a large Buddha belly. "I think he wore something like a 44-inch waist in order to accommodate it all. So the neighbors started calling him 'Tubby' when he was little."

"I get it. He was an imposing physical figure."

"Well, there is something else that I haven't told you." I paused.

"Tubby used to be a New Orleans cleaner when he was younger."

"Cleaner? So what? I mean, what is he going to do? Dry clean one of those people to death? Spray them with collar stiffener until they can't handle it any more? Tell them he won't get their stains out unless they are nice to him?"

"Not that type of cleaner."

"Then what?"

"A cleaner is as a hit man."

Now Christine looked at me like I was not only nuts, but also that I had a long beaked nose, big pointed ears, and two horns coming out of my head.

"How do you know?"

"Tubby told me one time while we he was sitting smoking his big joint."

"Were you freaked out?"

"Not really," I shrugged.

"Yea, that's normal. 'Hi, my name is Mr. Cleaner, may I babysit your children?'" She looked at me again as if I were Lucifer. But she was also curious to know more.

"I even asked Tubby about how he felt about doing what he did before."

Christine put her index finger on her chin like she was thinking, and then said jokingly with a fake, husky voice pretending to be Tubby:

"Yep, boy, used to wake myself up in the morning, kiss the kids on the cheeks, kiss the wife, drink some coffee, have some donuts, and then go to the house of the next guy I had to whack. And then, after, you know, after I cleaned up the entire skull and all of those little details, I'd go and have a nice cold ice cream sundae while sitting underneath a Norman Rockwell painting! I loved my job."

"Go ahead, I'm dying to hear this," she said sarcastically.

"We were sitting in the smoke-filled living room of Alby's house. I remember that Tubby had his shirt off and had a large chunk of grass that he was rolling into a joint on the table in front of him. Tubby used the couch as his bed when he slept at the house, and so the room was always full of his smoke. I was sitting on a chair across from him and, when I took a break from playing my Martin guitar, I kind of jumped in."

"What did you say?" Christine asked.

"I said, 'Tubby, can I ask you a question about what you did before?'" Tubby looked over at me with his wild eyes, as his hair stood straight up from having just woken up, and yet he calmly responded: "'Yea, baby, whatch you want to know?'"

"So I said, 'well, how did you feel about it? I mean the things you used to do to people for a living?'"

"He responded, 'I felt fine about it,' staring into my eyes like he was talking about digging ditches or operating a crane. 'All of dem mothafuckas had it coming. Dey took money dat wazn't deirs from the wrong mothafuckas. That's it. Plain and simple, baby.' He took a big drag off his joint."

"Disturbing," Christine said, taking a small sip of her wine.

"And I think all of the people across the street knew that fact about him."

"Scary," Christine said as she closed her eyes.

"I know. Plus," I continued, "one night, Tubby told me about the arsenal of weapons he had in precise detail: pistols, a sniper rifle, several submachine guns, and homemade silencers."

"My God, he must be the number one member of the National Rifle Association!" she said with a smirk.

"Tubby could be their poster child."

"But, in all seriousness, I bet this man had a tough life, right?" She poured some more wine into my glass and into hers. "Thank you," I said.

"Of course," she answered.

"On top of his father being locked up when he was younger, not going to high school, and having children as a young man, he told me one night how his nephew was killed by his sister."

I sipped my wine in preparation for the story.

"Tubby's sister was a heroin addict, along with her husband. They used to shoot their son up with the stuff." I slapped my arm. "Tubby told me his nephew was about 17 when his parents started getting him into it. One night, they were across the river in Algiers. They tried to shoot their son up with some strong stuff but they missed a vein. After that, the boy's heart stopped. He died instantly that night."

Christine looked at me for a few seconds. Her pupils were fixated on mine. I think she had no idea I was going to relay such a story to her. She took a sip of her Malbec.

"It's so sad," Christine said, with furrowed eyebrows as she put her hand over her mouth while looking at me. A tear came to her eye.

"My eyes were also tearing when Tubby told me the story," I said to Christine. "So I kind of understand why he smoked seriously strong grass every day, all day, from sunrise to sunset. I mean, when I would go visit Alby on business trips to New Orleans, I'd wake up with Alby to go to the coffee shop, say around 7 in the morning, and Tubby would be sitting there rolling his morning spliff."

"To forget and to numb himself, no doubt," Christine concluded.

"No question," I said to Christine when I jumped back into the conversation. "I mean, Tubby had supported three kids who were in public universities throughout the South, so I think he felt like he needed to keep it together for them. I think in an odd way the pot helped him to function."

"So he was trying?" She looked at me with hope.

"That was my impression," I nodded. "And so I learned from Tubby."

"How so?"

"He reminded me a little bit of the character in the movie *The Professional,*" I said. "Have you ever seen that?"

"No."

"In the movie, there is a hit man who takes a little girl under his arm after her parents die, and takes care of her for a period of time, until he is shot by the police."

"Wow," Christine said as she nodded her head in disbelief.

"What was cool about the movie was that the hit man had this other side which was caring and sensitive toward the girl. He had his dark side, but he didn't let it blot out his light and caring side. This duality made him endearing."

We paused and drank our wine.

"Who played the little girl? Which actress? I seem to picture her in my head, but I can't put a finger on her name," Christine asked.

"I think it was Nathalie Portman," I answered.

"And so how did Alby know Tubby?" Christine took a sip of her Malbec.

"Tubby was a patient of Alby's. After the treatment, they formed a friendship. I think Alby acted as a mentor to Tubby – to get him reformed and onto a more positive part of this life."

Christine and I were pretty buzzed at this point from the wine. I looked around at the paintings in her living room for a moment. And then Christine broke the silence:

"So going back to how you said Alby put on an act. How was it not an act?"

The number six stopped at its 59th Street stop. A slew of shoppers with bags from Bloomingdales came onto the subway car.

"You mean how was Alby seemingly powerless, but actually powerful?" I remember sipping some more wine.

She nodded.

"How was he the Jedi knight in disguise?" she asked.

"Maybe not a Jedi knight," I said, "because I only think there are about ten of those in the world, and I know he was not one of them."

"Cause he never pulled out his sword?"

"Oh yea, it just wasn't that big."

We laughed together.

"I ask because I often find myself hiding from who I am out of fear of rejection. I guess I kind of put on an act, too, in order to keep others at bay, especially after September eleventh," she said staring into my eyes as she took a sip of her wine. She was still hiding what she seemed to want to say, but couldn't let herself tell me.

I paused to think of how to describe Alby.

"Behind 'bruised ego' and his Lower Ninth Ward address, Alby had cash, investments, and powerful connections. He also knew so many people in that city, from restaurant owners to street merchants, all of whom he used to say hello to and who used to call out to him affectionately, 'yea you right, Alby.' He was a regular 'homeboy.' I mean, I remember one of his friends was this tough as nails 'coon ass.'"

"Meaning?"

"One of the Cajuns that grew up in the swamps. The coon ass, whose name was Jean- Pierre, had fought in the Korean War. He was lean, like one hundred and forty pounds, but was very muscular, knew martial arts, and worked out a bunch. He used to carry a .44 Magnum pistol around with him and a long hunting knife."

"They can do that in Louisiana?"

"If you have the right permit, and sometimes even if you don't, but if you know the parish police well enough."

"That's so foreign to my New York thinking," Christine said. "Do you want some more wine?"

"Yes, please. Thanks."

Christine then poured some more Malbec.

"My pleasure. Now, so what about these swamps?"

"Jean-Pierre knew where all of the good spots to find the alligators. The locals even named some of them. I remember going down there with Alby once to visit Jean Pierre, who told us how he used to swim in the swamps as a child with the other locals after their parents would properly feed the alligators."

"Crazy," Christine shook her head.

"Or courageous. Could you see a tough New Yorker, like some Brooklyn or Bronx guy, down there? He would shit in his pants swimming in those waters."

"I think anybody would shit in their pants swimming in those waters," Christine said. "Not those coon asses. So I doubted that any of the men in his neighborhood would have taken Alby lightly. He had the capability to . . . "

"Feed one of their legs to an alligator while the others watched?" Christine said as she took another sip of her wine. "I wish they had done that to the fuckers who did September 11th. Let the crawfish eat them when they sink to the bottom of the swamp for all I care. This water board stuff is rookie shit," she said in anger and frustration.

I was surprised at her comment.

"Among other things," I said, looking at her with raised eyebrows in response to her out of the blue comment.

"And yet you guys had a good time with another? I mean, you really spent a lot of time with Alby?"

"Yup. I was teaching junior college at the time at a place called Delgado. I think the locals called it 'Delga – Doo.' After I'd wake up in the morning, like around 10:00, he would come over. We would make fresh coffee, take it outside by the pool, roll a small joint, smoke, and read the morning *New York Times* or *Wall Street Journal*."

"Pool?"

"I lived in a house on Louisiana Avenue that had a pool in the back."

"Nice."

"It was usually so hot down there that you didn't want to be too far away from air conditioning or pool water. We'd usually invite some girlfriends over to swim with us in the mornings. We'd kind of party a lot during the day, and then I would teach junior college at night. Eventually, I got a more regular job downtown in the central business district."

"Sounds like fun," Christine said, as she took her back off the couch and leaned toward me a little more closely. "But maybe you had some demons you weren't facing?"

She stared point blank into my eyes. I took a sip of my wine, looked around her cozy living room, and purposely ignored her question.

"It was a blast. Most of our days started like that. I mean, we'd have lunch, take a siesta, and then I would start preparing for class."

"Did you guys go out at night?"

"Mostly. I mean, there is so much good music in New Orleans. Any night of the week you can go out and hear jazz, blues, rock and roll, gypsy, or hip-hop. The city has such a raffish charm that is hard to ignore."

"Is Alby pretty much all you hung out with in New Orleans for the few years you were down there?"

"Nope. Before I met Alby, I became real good friends with Luna Francis the woman who was my neighbor in New Orleans. She was such a trip, in a good way. She was also a courageous survivor."

"Want another splash of wine?"

"Please."

She poured a healthy splash for both of us and looked at me curiously. I felt like she wanted to know about Luna's courageousness. While Christine didn't know it, Luna, like Christine, had loss in her life that she was learning to deal with. After a short pause, Christine I remember Christine asking:

"So what was Luna like?"

I remember looking back at Christine and wondering how to describe Luna. The number six train was now at the 51st Street stop.

CHAPTER 28

Surrogate Sister

"I think the best place to start is to tell you that when Luna was 23, whose one brother died alone in some cabin in Colorado," I recall saying to Christine.

"Alone?" Christine asked aghast. "What?"

"Right," I nodded my head.

"That's horrible." Christine put a hand over her mouth and then took it off. "What happened?"

"I don't know much more than that," I shrugged my shoulders. "I don't think Luna liked talking about it too much."

"I understand," Christine said. "Well, tell me more about her, Jack."

"She was about five foot five with thick, curly brown hair that goes down to her shoulders. She had stunning pale rider blue eyes and paper white skin with freckles."

"Did she have any tattoos?"

"Yes."

"I'm thinking about getting a tattoo, which is why I asked. Is she thin?"

"She was Victorian pretty. I remember when I lived next to her . . ."

"You lived next to her?"

"Yup," I nodded, "across the street. When I came back from traveling in Italy and other places, I lived across the street from her in New Orleans."

"Got it," she took a sip of her wine. "Where is her family originally from?"

"Salem, Massachusetts. One of her ancestors, Amber, was an alleged witch who fled Salem and eventually snuck into a San Francisco Catholic church disguised as a nun in order to beat a murder rap – only to get charged with another one. Luna was quietly powerful the same way."

"This Amber character sounds super boring," Christine said deadpan. "And what about her immediate family?"

"She seemed like she was super close with her mom and dad." I sipped my wine and shrugged. "After I left New Orleans to move to New York, Luna sold her house and her business to move to Copenhagen."

"Business?"

"She owned a book store in Pirate's Alley in New Orleans which had a coffee shop in front and old-school hair salon in back. I used to go there to buy books, get my haircuts from her, and drink coffee."

"And moved to where in Copenhagen?" Christina asked, intrigued.

"I think somewhere in the center of town. She bought a condo there, in an upscale part of the city."

"Did she know anybody there?"

"Not one soul."

"Wow. I don't think I could have done that. There would have been too much of the unknown for me to face. It would have scared me."

"Like walking around the bedroom at night without the lights on?" I asked sarcastically. "Kind of like that," she retorted matching my tone. "But I think it would be more like swimming at night in the ocean without moonlight or anything else to give you an idea of what is around you. More like that!"

"Pretty gutsy, I agree," I said.

"Did she work while she was down there?"

"Not really. I think for two years she just had a good time."

"Two years?" Christine asked with surprise.

"Two years," I responded with a nod.

"She must have had a blast," Christine said with a smirk.

"I think she did. When I was in Copenhagen on my trip . . . " "Was she there with you?"

"No, I went there after hearing from her how nice it was."

"Got it," Christine raised her glass in a cheers type of way and then took a sip. I did the same with my wine.

"I mostly saw very tall blond women and men. So she must have stood out with her dark curly hair and shorter stature. 'I love that city,' she would always tell me about Copenhagen."

"You went for vacation?"

"No, I had a client there. A painter. He painted Vikings."

"Huh?"

"Vikings were Scandinavian pirates who sailed as far as Sicily and Morocco in the middle of the night."

"So what was it like in Copenhagen?"

"I saw why she loved the city so much. It has an almost perfect mix of Danish order with a little bit of Viking rascal underneath. It was very eclectic."

"How so?"

"Take the women. They would either dress very conservative . . . " "Like Barbra Bush?" she asked with a wry smile.

"Kind of, but then some would mix some of that into something a little more funky – picture a woman wearing a summer dress with espadrilles and a stylish necklace from the local museum."

"Classic with a twist."

"I think that's why I felt comfortable with Luna when I moved back to New Orleans. I knew her taste. I had a feeling of where she stood. There was no second-guessing with her about her intentions and where she stood. She was, as my mother said once, my surrogate sister."

"What was one of your most memorable times down there with her? By the way, the bottle is almost finished," Christine said as she picked it up from the mahogany coffee table. "Shall we finish it?"

"Why not?" I answered.

Christine poured the last drops of the large bottle into our glasses. We were pretty toasted at this point.

The number six train was now at its 42nd Street stop.

"So what was a memorable time?" Christine asked as she apparently sought to live vicariously through my stories.

"Dressing up and going out on Halloween," I said wryly. "Where did you guys go?"

"The French Quarter. We got on our cruisers and headed down Magazine Street, a main drag of New Orleans filled with local clothing shops and restaurants."

"It must have been a zoo down there, no?"

"It was. Costumes, humidity, and the smell of alcohol saturated the streets. That pretty much sums up the quarter on Halloween night. Luna and I biked though this morass of people and alcohol like we were salmon swimming upstream. Magazine, then Bourbon Street, and on to Frenchmen Street!"

"Frenchman Street?"

"It's like the artist district there, like what So Ho used to be. When we got there, we saw feathers, boas, top hats, clown faces, tuxedos, doctors, lawyers, homeless drunks, make-up, fake nails, good looking women, ugly men, burnt out college students, burnt out college drop outs, skanks, bartenders, Southern frat boys and girls, lost souls, and tourists."

"What about giraffes and tigers?" she asked with humor.

"Pretty much any type you could find in a larger city like New York, you could find within a few blocks in the Quarter on Halloween night."

"'Shit, this place is packed!' I remember saying to her as we rode with the slight, humid wind from the Mississippi in our faces."

"I love it," Christine said.

"'How about going somewhere a little bit less crowded?' I remember asking Luna," I said as I looked at Christine.

"'Naw, let's stay here and get into it a little more,' Luna said to me."

"That's one thing I loved about being with her," I said to Christine. "She opened my eyes to another world that I might not have been courageous enough to enter if it weren't for her."

I then paused.

"Or, more accurately," I continued, as I took another sip of wine, "I think she helped me keep my eyes open at a time when I was scared to keep them open."

"You are lucky to have had people like Alby and Luna in your life," Christine said. "I wish I had people like that who are there for me. You know, loved ones who have courage in ways that I don't have."

Christine paused reflectively.

The number six train was now stopped at 33rd Street. "So what did you all do?"

"We stayed in the middle of the crowd of people – and I loved it! People would brush up against me every second with different costumes and different facial expressions: distraught, elated, tortured, and content. It was in this tidal wave of people that I felt like I was truly experiencing New Orleans on Halloween."

"It's odd that she chose a place like Copenhagen to relocate after living in such a colorful spot," Christine commented after she sipped her wine.

"Actually, I think Copenhagen and New Orleans have a lot in common. They both have an emphasis on tradition, like their restaurants and their sense of history," I explained.

"How so?" Christine asked. "I mean, I've never been to either place. But I love hearing about them. Perhaps someday I'll gather up enough courage to travel to these places."

"You will," I told her confidently and then paused. "To give you an idea, I remember going to eat dinner at Bibendum, Copenhagen's oldest wine bar, no Internet connection, right by where Luna bought her apartment."

"Old school. No Internet!"

"Totally. I remember there was a table on my right with a slew of people around 70 to 80. They seemed to be having fun. In spite of their age, and whatever problems they might have encountered in their life, they were there laughing with one another."

"I bet," Christine said.

"At the left half of the table sat the men – the right, the women," I moved my hands right and left to emphasize my point. "They spoke Danish so I had no idea what they were saying most of the time. But their expressions spoke louder than their words. They were all smiling. The men hit one another in their shoulders as they talked politics, relationships, and whatever else. I remember how their voices rose and fell in tone with the subject matter of the talk:

'Hey!'

'Non!'

'Pardon!'

'Excuse!'

"They sat around the table as though they were in an informal caucus – an Indian pow- wow of sorts right next to me. The women weren't much different than the men except their highs and lows were not as drastic."

"I wonder what they were talking about -- sex, politics, music, death, life, grandchildren, hair loss, or, perhaps, all of the above?" Christine asked.

"Whatever it was, I felt a certain amount of security in their presence. It was as though their brief looks towards my direction and around the restaurant said: 'If we can make it, so can you.'"

"Were those people married?"

"All of them looked like they were. I think a lot of them had rings on their ring fingers, or they just looked like they had been in relationships for a long time. They reminded me of the professors that I encountered at the University of Chicago. The older ones, that is. Their gray hair and wrinkled skin had many stories to tell – and much advice to give."

"Like?" Christine asked.

I paused to think for a second.

The number six train stopped at and just left its 28th Street stop.

"I think stuff like 'money is important, but relationships are more important.'"

"And you feel like many in New Orleans, or maybe even in Chicago, have the same sentiments?" Christine asked.

"I think so. People in New Orleans don't care as much about money, which is perhaps why . . . "

"Louisiana is one of the poorest states in the nation?" Christine interrupted.

"Maybe. But the good thing is that people don't always ask you what you do and where you live as soon as they meet you there. Whereas in New York, that is the first thing people usually have to say to one another."

"Depending on where you are, and with whom," she pointed out.

"I guess I am just speaking in general, broad-brush terms. Perhaps Manhattan is more like that, but it depends on who you hang with there, too," I conceded.

"So, going back to that restaurant in Copenhagen, what did you think of tradition? I mean, your sense of it?" Christine asked. Like me, I could sense she was looking for some type of stability in her life after observing the disheveled nature of her apartment that looked like she had just moved in. Furniture was scattered all over the place. Dresser drawers were open, furniture was covered in plastic, and she had thrown pieces of clothing all over the place. And yet I felt like she felt like she was home already. I, too, felt very at home with Christine in her disheveled apartment.

"The people at the table were courageous enough to strive for the best that they thought they could get in life, even though the best might not have been obtainable right away, that day,

that moment, or that year. They were the types from that older generation who didn't seem to give up at the slightest sign of adversity, and all the while knowing that they may not necessarily get where they are aiming for – but pretty close."

"But it is the intention that counts," Christine pointed out. "What is that phrase, shoot for the moon, and, even if you miss, you'll land among the stars? It goes something like that."

She took a long sip of her wine.

The six train continued from the 23rd Street stop.

"It takes courage to have those sentiments especially in today's world. It seems to be full of divorces and cynicism, particularly in big cities like New York," she continued.

"It seems that way," I agreed. "Perhaps there is just as much in smaller towns, but maybe it's easier to avoid than it is here; New York seems to be more about self."

"Then why did you want to come back to New York, Jack?" Christine asked in a serious tone. "Why didn't you just stay in New Orleans?"

It seemed that Christine was asking this question of herself, just as much as she was asking it of me.

CHAPTER 29

Don't Ignore Pantyhose Runs

"I came back to try to confront my demons." I took some more Malbec into my mouth, swooshed it around, and then swallowed it.

"I wanted to come back and do this city on my terms. I think being with people like Alby and Luna gave me courage to come back here. With them, I felt a certain safety and grounding which gave me strength to come back. And yet, I felt like I was not on the right path down there for the long term. I felt like I took a step . . . "

"Backwards?" Christine jumped in to say.

"Right. Backwards." I took another sip of wine. "But maybe sometimes you have to take a step back from trees so you can see the forest."

"Good for you, Jack. I can appreciate that. Do you have much stuff to move?"

"Just two bags of clothes. I feel like a commando."

She giggled.

"How did you end up in New York?" I asked.

"I was a philosophy major and studied art after school. I am originally from upstate New York, but I felt like New York City would be the best place for me to explore the arts to and to face some demons that I myself have had. I actually just moved into this place."

"Let's check out the upstairs."

"Sounds good," I said.

We got up and went up the creaky stairs to see the room for rent. It was a Victorian looking space with ornate designs on the corners – something that you would see in the far West, in the country somewhere, but was instead here in the middle of Brooklyn.

"Nice," I said.

"Yea, it's real cute. My bedroom is over there," she pointed her finger through the door to the bedroom across the hallway. That bedroom, too, looked like a Victorian enclave – a large bed in the middle of the room, fluffy comforter good for late Saturday morning sleeping, and a large iron bedpost.

"The room is $1,000. That includes all utilities. I would need one month security deposit before you move in."

"Let me think about it. I haven't been back in New York that long and I want to explore my options."

"I understand. Take your time," she said.

We started back down the stairs. We were visited again by the creaks normally heard in a horror movie when the villain is crawling up – or down – the stairs, creak, step, creak, step, creak.

When we arrived at the bottom of the stairs, I asked her: "Did you have dinner?"

"Didn't have dinner yet," she said.

"It would be great to go to the diner together just around the corner – by the subway stop. Does that sound good?" I asked.

"I love that diner. Let's do it!"

I sat on the creaky velvet couch as she put on her scarf, boots, and sweater. As we left the apartment, I felt kind of sad. I loved the place and her energy. I just didn't know if I wanted to live there. Christine had this calming effect on me without all of the numbness that comes with taking anti-anxiety medicine.

By now, the number six train had stopped at, and left, its 14th Street/Union Square stop. We left the apartment. The air outside was cool on the fall night, kind of like the bone-chilling air that I used to encounter in New Orleans. We were not far from the East River. The breeze came through the trees and lightly brushed our faces. As we walked by a subway entrance in Brooklyn Heights, she said softly to me:

"I fell there a few days ago," pointing to the rain drenched steps. "What happened?"

"I went to break my fall, and I somehow almost broke my nose on the rail. I guess my guard was down, and I wasn't paying attention. So when my feet fell out from under me, I tried to grab the rail but instead of my hands grabbing it, my nose did!"

As she told me this, I envisioned her sharp slightly crooked nose grabbing onto the rail, not being able to support the weight of her body, and cracking. I had little goose pimples all over me when I thought about her pain. We continued our walk under the tear-dropped trees of Brooklyn Heights.

"I guess I didn't tell you earlier, but it has been five years since my father was killed on September 11th."

"No, you didn't."

"I've been holding it inside me and haven't told many people about it. I never wanted to accept that I would never see him again. I kept working, hooking up with random guys, and smoking and drinking a lot. Whatever it took. I was running away from his death and from myself. And then I moved back to New York City so that I could face it all. And yet, I didn't want to – even when I got here."

"But the blood," she went on, "from my nose was something I could not run away from like I did from my father's death. The blood just gushed out and I could not stop it, other than by

later putting a cloth over it. Then the feelings, which I had suppressed so long, came out about my father. I could not control them either."

She paused to look over at me to see if I was listening, and my eyes assured her I was.

She looked back in front of her.

"I usually try to control my feelings so that they will not get the better of me. I couldn't do it this time. So I just sat there with my knees to my chest on the wet, desolate, subway stairway. Tears were running down my face. Blood ran from my nose to the edge of my chin and then down my shirt on to the rain water."

"How did you handle the pain, I mean, didn't you want to get right to a hospital?"

"In an odd way, it felt so good. I was relieved. I had never really let that side of myself out before. I have been trapping myself thinking that part of myself was not me – but someone other than me, a past me, another me, someone I did not associate myself with – emotional, sensitive . . . "

"Human?" I interrupted.

"Yes, perhaps you could even say that. Breaking my nose was something that allowed that part of me to get out. It was a like a prison break for the imprisoned me."

We arrived at the diner. It was the type of diner that you would find in the 1950s – neon signs, strong black coffee, a warm, local owner named Vito, good hamburgers, local truckers sitting next to local mothers sitting next to local accountants at the counter. It was a comfortable, no frills atmosphere.

As the six train left its Astor Place stop, I remembered back to the waiter who served us at the diner.

"May I help you?" The waiter said. He an WASP looking man who had the physical characteristics of Woody Allen as well as his demeanor – timid, awkward, and smart. A crease appeared on his already wrinkled–piece-of-paper face when he saw Christine's broken nose.

"What happened to you, baby?"

"I cracked my nose."

"Honey, I can see that! You need a home cooked meal. Come on in and let me seat you."

We walked with the Woody Allen looking waiter over to our booth and sat down. The seats were typical diner. On a hot humid day, the backs of your sweaty legs would get stuck and would leave trails of dampness. Menus were in front of us. All of the usual suspects were there – hamburger, fries, Coke. We sat and stared at the menus for a bit until a waitress whose name could have been Norma or Betty or Bianca approached us – hair in a bun, chewing gum, pencil in hand, notepad ready to go:

"What'll you have?"

"Burger, fries, and Coke, please," I said.

"Sure. And you, miss?" the waitress asked Christine. "I'll have the same, please."

"Do you come here often?" I asked Christine. "Once in a blue moon."

"So you told me a little about your family on the way over here and about your pop.

What about your mother?"

At that point, the waitress came by with our Cokes. "Thank you, miss," I said to the waitress.

"You are welcome. Burgers and fries will be up in a minute," the waitress said and left.

"My mother is a Republican mayor of a small town in upstate New York. But I'm not a Republican," Christine said as she sipped her Coke.

"Were you angry after the eleventh? I mean with what happened to your father and all." I sipped my Coke.

"Yes, I was angry at him, at the killers, at the country, at the world."

"So why did you come back to New York City? I mean, didn't you like living upstate? It's far away from all of that," I pointed my finger towards the former World Trade Center site. "Maybe it would have been easier to deal with your anger back upstate?"

"No, I needed to come back. I needed to see where it happened. It helped me."

"I get it. After my brother Liam died in a car accident, my mother would visit his grave and put fresh flowers on it every week. She still does. I think it helps her."

"I bet it does," Christine agreed. "And your father? How did he cope?" At that point, the waitress came back:

"Here you go, fresh burgers and fries," the waitress said with a thick Brooklyn accent.

"Thank you," Christine said to the waitress.

"Other than the day that they buried Liam, my father has never visited Liam's grave," I said as I chewed on some fries. "In a way, I totally understand why he doesn't."

"Why?"

"Well, I went a few times with my mother," I said after I finished a bite of my burger, "and it felt very depressing."

"That is exactly why I did not want to come back to New York City. To me, the city was like a big cemetery after September eleven. But I needed to come back."

"Me, too. I felt like I needed to come back here. I have been running from myself, too." We paused as we ate.

"But I wonder if running really leads you anywhere, other than deeper into the problems you are running from," I thought out loud. "It's like the more you run from your demons, the worse they become?"

Christine listened and then jumped in.

"It reminds me of a quote from August Wilson, the late playwright. It goes something like, um, let me see: 'Confront the dark parts of yourself and work to banish them with illumination and forgiveness. Your willingness to wrestle with your demons will cause your angels to sing. Use the pain as fuel, as a reminder of your strength.'" She then sipped her Coke.

"And so I felt like," she continued, "I needed to try to wrestle with my demons not only with illumination and forgiveness, but also with caring and nurturing. I mean, our demons are things on the inside that need care and tending to, not anger. I think the demons come about when we face uncertainties in life, whatever they may be. They make us doubt ourselves, and question our own self worth. I found that anger just made my demons worse, like when I was living outside of New York City."

"I guess its like a pantyhose run. The more you go about your day and ignored it, the worse it becomes."

She giggled. I took another bite of my burger as some three or so fun, rowdy Brooklyn kids came in to the diner. They looked like the friends I used to hang with growing up in Los Angeles – messy hair, dirty hands from skating all day, wearing Vans, and always carrying their boards. I dipped some French fries into the ketchup.

"Maybe the anger allows us to avoid the issue. Maybe it takes courage to actually face up to what the issue is?" I asked skeptically.

Christine nodded to me with an "affirmative."

At that point, we finished our meal at the diner and I paid for the bill. As I started walking Christine back to her apartment, we remained generally silent. It was a comfortable silence. It was the type of calming silence that you get in a forest with the sun peaking through the trees on a cool, crisp, fall afternoon.

"You don't need to walk me home. It's a good neighborhood."

"Are you sure? I'd be happy to."

"For sure."

"I had better be heading back to where I am staying anyway – the kids get to sleep early and I don't want to wake them. It's such a nice home there – Alby's sister is so warm."

"You'll find the same warm home one day," Christine said with an affectionate smile. "Just let me know if you want the apartment."

"Of course, I'll call you in the coming week."

We said our goodbyes and gave one another a hug. I didn't end up taking the apartment.

At that point in my memories of Christine, the number six train I was riding had arrived at my Bleeker Street stop downtown. I got up and headed upstairs to Bleeker Street. I started walking back towards my apartment on Bleeker Street through the crowds and noise in Greenwich Village. When I got into my apartment, it was about 6:00 p.m. in the evening. I took my shoes off, lay down on my couch to take a nap, and had a vivid dream.

CHAPTER 30

Freezing Chicago Rain

"Think back to the showers that Maja told you about," Ace, my inner voice, hinted in my dream.

"What?" I said to him.

In my dream, Ace was wearing his trademark tuxedo. He was again sitting on the jet- black, Chesterfield couch in The Chicago Society library. A powerful and cold Chicago rain tumbled down on the windows behind him. It was about midnight in Chicago. Other than the pounding rain and the panting of his black Labrador retrievers, the room was quiet. I was sitting on a wooden chair across from him. The only light was a white candle on the black, mid-century modern looking mahogany coffee table in front of him. He turned his pale blue eyes upon me.

"You mean Aron and Maja, the ones I met at the writing course after I met Christine?" I asked him.

"Right," he nodded. "Why?" I asked.

"People can be courageous one day but then be uncourageous the next day. So there is something more to wrestling with your demons than merely having courage, Jack. In other words, don't be deluded into thinking that courage is the silver bullet, assuming there is *a* silver bullet," he said with a smile.

Around 8:00 p.m., the siren of a police car screaming down Bleeker Street woke me. I got up, opened the CD player, and inserted the jazz album *Kind of Blue* by Miles Davis. I went back to lie down on my couch. As I lay there looking up at the ceiling and listening to the first song on the album, "So What?", I thought back to Aron and his wife, Maja, who was a holocaust survivor. I met them a year or so after moving back to New York. I was 32 years old at the time.

(F) PERSEVERANCE

CHAPTER 31

A Fresh Shower

"They led the prisoners into a dressing room with the promise of a fresh shower. Of course, the prisoners gladly took their clothes off. Most of the prisoners wore the six-pointed Star of David, but some of the more rebellious ones proudly wore a cocktail of symbols – one for being a Jew, one for being a 'race defiler,' one for being a recidivist, one for being a criminal against the Reich, and one for being a homosexual, even if the person wasn't a homosexual!"

Maja Bethe looked over to me with a sly, defiant smile and then gazed back down at the children playing with their mothers in Central Park. We were sitting on the balcony of her penthouse apartment, which she shared with her husband, Aron Bethe, on the Upper West Side. It was Sunday morning around 10:30 a.m.

"After they got naked, they were led into the showers. Once they were in, the doors were closed and they were gassed with Zyklon B, a form of cyanide. They dropped to the shower floor like human flies."

When Maja told me this story, she didn't seem to blink.

"The Nazi soldiers pulled out the prisoners' gold teeth. Then they threw the poisoned bodies into the ovens to be cremated. Each concentration camp competed with the other in terms of killing efficiency and profit. Some camps, such as the one in Birkenau, could gas to death as many as 2,000 people a day. Throughout my life, I have imagined myself going through the same steps that these prisoners took when they were led to their deaths. I could have been one of them. But I was lucky."

She then turned and looked at me.

Maja stood about five foot five. She was born not long before the start of World War II. Her hair, like her eyes, was sandy brown. Her short hair and small hoop earrings framed her slightly wrinkled skin. Her hands shook ever so slightly when she moved them. Her style and spirit were both very elegant. She often wore colorful Hermes scarves around her neck. She always wore a put-together outfit – bracelets, nice wool pants, a turtleneck, sometimes a beret. I first met Maja and Aron in a writing course at New York University ("NYU"). They always sat in the front row. I remember the first time I met them:

"Do you guys ride a moped or motorcycle to class?" I asked her one night during the start of class. "I see that you both carry helmets."

"Yes. We have a Vespa that we ride from home," Maja said. "Where do you all live?" I asked.

"Upper West Side. And you?" Maja asked.

"I live on Bleeker Street. What's your name?"

"Maja. And yours?"

"Jack."

We shook hands.

"This is my husband, Aron," Maja said with a bright smile as she pointed to Aron.

"Hello, Jack," Aron put his hand out. When I shook it, his hand gripped mine very firmly.

Aron's gray beard went down to the middle of his chest. What remained of his thinning hair was gray, too. He was about five foot six, but people took notice of him when he entered a room. He wore clear, Danish eyeglass frames, fancied Panerai diving watches, and usually wore black pants along with a black or gray turtleneck. Born in Heidelberg, Germany, on September 4, 1939, he spoke with a slight German accent. Some of his family migrated to the U.S. after the war, to places like New York, New Orleans, and Los Angeles. His eyes were deep set; when he looked at you, you could see that he had a clear picture in his mind of what he thought about you.

He was a sprightly breath of fresh air in the class.

"With your writing," the professor explained in class one time, "you don't want to be predictable. I mean, we all know how the U.S., for example, always supports Israel in pretty much any move it makes. Your writing should be a little more unpredictable than that," she said, smirking.

I remember Aron raising his hand. "Yes, Aron," the professor said.

"So what you are saying is that our writing should be more unpredictable, like the Chicago weather?" As Aron said this, he had a satisfied smirk.

"Well," the professor backtracked, "I am not going that far." They often had little skirmishes like this.

"She goes too far," Aron confided to me one time, "with her infusion of political views in class. She should keep them to herself."

I smiled in response. He shot a mischievous grin back at me. I loved this man. It made sense he was a "troublemaker." He told me once how some of his family, like a woman named Sophia Gordon (born Bethe), from New Orleans, ended up fighting in the French Resistance during WWII.

After class one night a few days later, I approached Aron and Maja: "Would you guys like to have a bite to eat?"

"Sure, Jack," Maja said, "that would be nice."

We went to a hip little Japanese sushi café around the corner from NYU campus to have dinner. We sat down next to the entrance. "Sweet Virginia," a song from The Rolling Stones album *Exile on Main Street*, was playing in the background.

On the walls were posters of various kinds, including a movie poster for *Pulp Fiction*, and another for the punk band The Ramones. The restaurant was crowded with NYU students of different types: some preppies wearing Top Siders, some gothic metal fans, and some students who looked like they read chemistry on Friday nights, too. The place boomed with laughter, clinging glasses, and loud music.

I didn't think a couple as old as Maja and Aron would appreciate a place this loud. But they did not seem like your typical couple. They may have been old in age, but they were young at heart. I kind of jumped in with questions I had wanted to ask all semester, but didn't have the opportunity to.

CHAPTER 32

Especially These Days

"So where did y'all meet?"

"In the Israeli military," Maja answered. "My mother and I escaped the Holocaust from Yugoslavia. Eventually, I ended up in Israel, where I joined the military. It was there that I met Aron."

I looked over at Aron, who was sitting next to Maja, and asked him:

"Do you remember what you were doing, Aron, when you first met her?"

"Let me see, if I remember correctly, I was working on a missile guidance system," he answered as he pulled the menu closer to look at it.

"And, you, Maja?"

"I was in Israeli intelligence," she said as she also pulled her menu closer. "Mossad?" I asked.

"Well, not technically, but a related organization within the military that shared intelligence with Mossad."

"And you, Jack, what about you," Aron asked after he put the menu down. "Are you married? A girlfriend? Or at least a lover?"

"Not now. I have found it kind of hard to meet women in this city. Of course, there are a lot of women here. But it seems that many are in a rush to get a boyfriend, get the ring, get married and have kids. And yet, it seems, they get divorced before you know it," I said matter- of-factly as I looked at the menu. "I guess I feel like marriage has turned into a racket," and then looked up to ask, "How long have you guys been married?"

Maja looked at Aron, and Aron looked at Maja, and then Aron looked at me, "It's hard to believe, but I think its been close to fifty years."

"Fifty years! I can't believe it. Wow!" My eyebrows raised and my forehead wrinkled with disbelief and also some relief.

So they do exist I said to myself. Couples that stay together do exist! "Fifty years, and I can't believe it either," Aron said shaking his head.

"I think I could probably count on my hands the number of people I have met who have been married that long," I said.

"Especially these days," Maja said, looking at me seriously. "Why do you think that is so, Maja?" I asked.

A tattooed waitress came by to take our orders. The short, stout, rock n' roll Japanese woman spoke with a thick Japanese accent:

"Are you ready to, ah, orda?"

"Yes, please," Aron responded. "Jack, go first."

"No. Maja, please go first," I said.

"I guess chivalry isn't dead," Maja said with an appreciative smile. "I'll have a spicy tuna roll, please, and a glass of iced water."

"Okay," the waitress said with a nod. "Go ahead, Jack," Aron said.

"Thank you. I'll have a California roll, please, and a Kirin beer."

"Same here," Aron said, as he handed over the menus to the waitress.

"A few reasons," Maja said in answer to my earlier question, not missing a beat. "But I think the biggest one is instant gratification. People want things to happen now – love, wealth, knowledge."

"Do you think it's because of technology?" I asked.

The waitress came back and put the beers and water on the table. "Thank you," Aron said to the waitress.

"That certainly has made things move faster," Maja said after she put her water down. "But I wouldn't blame it all on technology. Guns don't kill people. People kill people. The same is true with technology. It can bring people together if used in the right way. But, if it is not used the right way, then you have people in their own little virtual worlds. Ever been to a coffee house where everyone seems to be on a personal device?" She opened the palm of her right hand to emphasize the point.

"Yes, totally," I nodded.

"It looks like they might as well as be in their own apartments. They are there, next to other people, but they are *not* living in the moment. Instead, their heads are in the virtual world. People used to live in the country, then they moved to the cities, and now they live in the virtual world."

"So technology is not the cause of the instant gratification?" I asked eagerly, leaning ever so slightly toward her.

"It could be," Maja thought out loud as she angled her head to the right and looked at me. "But I think the real reason is that people don't know how to persevere. They want things to come easy, now, now, now, sooner, sooner, now!"

She took a quick sip of her water and then proceeded.

"They don't think things will be hard. And, if something is hard, they don't want to deal with it. Yes, they may be courageous one day. They may do something that takes some guts. But many lose their determination after that. It's as if they feel they have met their quota, and that they are now entitled to have things come easily." She used her right index finger to point right and left – the right being the quota, the left being the easy life. "Life is not like that. Courage often requires persistence – every day, every week, every year. Otherwise, you make a gain one day only to lose it the next."

"Kind of like, um, kicking a drug habit?" I asked.

"You could say that. You quit one day, go to rehab, and then you seem fine for a couple of weeks, or even years. But then you slip at a party, take a little of something here, something there, and then you are back where you started. It might have been courageous of you to face your addiction and try to do something about it. But, to carry it through, you need to persevere. And that requires dogged persistence," she leaned forward with a furrowed brow driving her point home.

"A certain amount of vigilance?" I asked. "Right," Maja nodded. "Like standing guard."

"Perhaps it's because things aren't as hard now as during the war. I mean, things have been relatively quiet in the world compared to the World Wars, and so people have gotten kind of . . . "

"Spoiled," Maja interjected.

"A little." I nervously sipped my beer thinking I might be one of those spoiled ones. "People graduate from college and expect to have a job."

"That expectation is not realistic," Aron interjected. "You not only have to be smart, you also need to be persistent. Plenty of smart people in the world haven't done much with their lives because they don't have the resolve to carry things through," he said as he sipped his Kirin. "Others may not be as smart but they are bullish with their lives. They get things done. Of course, some luck is involved, too," he smiled.

"It sounds like you are speaking from personal experience. I mean, what was your life like here in New York when you first arrived?" I asked and then ate one of my California rolls with chopsticks.

"We lived in a rat hole of an apartment," Maja answered with a small smile using her chopsticks to eat one of her spicy tuna pieces.

"I wouldn't say that," Aron chimed in. "I would say it was more of a pin prick than a hole," as he smiled and then ate one of his rolls.

Maja wiped her mouth:

"We didn't have much. Aron and I worked hard, saved, and went through a lot of lean years before we moved out of our old apartment."

"Do you think people generally stick together like that now?" I asked after I took a sip of Kirin.

I noticed that the music in the background had now changed to the song "Sweet Black Angel" by The Stones.

"Not at all," Maja said. "It seems, from my impression after speaking with my daughter about her dating life, that people nowadays want to know where things are going to go, how they are going to go, and when they are going to go, right from the outset. It's like people don't want to take any time any more with things. At the first sign of trouble, or tough times, I get the impression that people are ready to bail," she said pointing out the window with her right thumb.

"Like the addict who goes into relapse?" I asked.

"Just like the addict. He starts, goes to rehab," Aron put the palm of his right hand flat on the table to as to indicate this stage, "and things go smoothly. But when the first rough patch comes along," he moved his hand to the right to indicate this stage, "he is back at the booze, or whatever it is he escapes into," Aron said.

"Is your daughter married?" I ate another piece of my roll. "Yes. And we have a granddaughter," Maja answered. "Lovely!" I said.

"Yes, it has been," she said.

"I guess I wonder if I am on the right path when it comes to women," I said in a confidingly. "I moved here with a French girlfriend and that didn't work out, to say the least. We moved very fast. We went from being friends, more or less, to lovers, and then, all of a sudden, to living with one another and then moving to New York in a matter of a year or so," I made a circular motion with my chopsticks to show the timeline around a clock I had drawn in the air.

"A whirlwind," Maja observed.

"Yes. And, in the end, while it did not end well, I learned to not be in such a rush to get things done, and that part of the fun is actually taking the time to get to know the other person – their likes, fears, dislikes, and all that." I ate another piece of my roll as some gothic girls with high-pitched voices wearing all black – Cure t-shirts, Doc Martin boots, eye shadow, and finger nail polish – walked into the grungy restaurant.

"I think the same thing is true about conquering your inner demons, whatever they are," Maja answered as she pointed to my chest with her index finger. "It takes courage, but it also takes persistence. Every day when you wake up, whether you like it or not, I think you have to face those dark parts of yourself and confront them."

"I never really thought about it that way." As I said this, I looked at the soy sauce on the table and reflected on my smoking habit, and how it might have been a way to avoid those dark parts.

"Jack, may I say something?" Maja interrupted my thoughts. "Yes, of course, Maja," I said hopefully.

"Take your time. Time shouldn't be a four-letter word. It has become one," she said looking directly into my eyes.

"Right," I nodded.

"Time can be your friend, not your enemy, when it comes to relationships – whether it is a relationship with a woman, a friend, or in your relationship with yourself. Things don't happen overnight – don't think they do," she said raising her eyebrows to emphasize the point.

"But I feel like that is what popular culture has to say. Get rich quick, get to the American dream tomorrow and own the house you have always wanted with no money down. Get the ring, get the wife, have the babies, or else you aren't an adult!" I exclaimed in a challenging tone.

"It does say that," nodding to express her agreement. But," she said with emphasis, "sometimes, it is good to take the path less traveled. Being an adult often requires doing just that," Maja pointed her index finger on the dinner table.

"Not following the sheep?" I responded.

"Right," Aron interjected after he wiped his face with the napkin. "Maybe it's the path that the sheep don't know about, or maybe they know about it, but they are afraid to take it, because some of it requires them to be alone."

"What do you mean?" I finished my sushi roll.

Aron put his chopsticks down and looked up at me. The restaurant music had changed from The Stones to The Doors. Their song, "People Are Strange," started playing.

"We live in a culture where people think life is going to be just like college – parties, connections, career," Aron said as he put out his left hand and flicked out his thumb, index finger, and middle finger. "It is not." He put his hand down. "A lot of times, you will have to sit there alone on the beach with your eyes closed and mind open," he paused to close his eyes and then opened them back up again, "as long as you need to, and reflect on what is important to you before you head back into the maze of the city, or wherever it is you are."

"So the silence of solitude allows you to reflect on a deeper level what is important?" I wondered out loud.

"Yes, exactly," Aron nodded in agreement.

"But being alone can be painful. It gets lonely. I mean, I miss having a girlfriend. I think it's been like six years since the French one," I said.

"I think being alone is different than being lonely. When you are alone, you can learn more about yourself, who you are about, what you like and don't like, and what is important to you. It's harder to do that when you are surrounded by the fashion, finance, and fun of a city like New York," Aron said grinning as he twirled his right index finger to make a circular motion in the air, mimicking my earlier motion.

"So the pain can be an ally?" I asked with a surprised tone.

"Yes," Aron said. "Just as time can be a painful friend. As you get older, you have less time to live," he quickly pointed to his watch with his right finger, "so this makes you think more about what is important to you – and what is not. I think the pain of time is there to help you, not hurt you."

"I think Aron is right," Maja chimed in, like a tag team member in a wrestling match. "Let time guide you, Jack, not scare you, like it does with so many people. Part of persevering is overcoming adversity now and into the future. It's almost like the adversity

makes you stronger," she pounded her chest with her right fist to emphasize the point.

"Like some philosopher said, 'What doesn't kill you makes you stronger,'" I said with my hand on my chin.

"Yes, I think there is something to what he was saying," Maja concluded. The Japanese rock n' roll waitress came by:

"Anything else?" she asked.

"I'll have some green tea, please," Maja said. "Me, too, please," Aron said.

"Yes, one for me, too. Thank you," I said.

"Ok, I'll be right back," the waitress said.

"Things are not perfect in life," Maja said as she turned her attention back to me. "Many think they are, especially in this country, with its immense wealth. But things work sometimes, don't work at others, need to be fixed, oiled, worked on, and the like. That is precisely what satisfaction is about. It should give you satisfaction to persevere over adversity, but only by going through the adversity can you get there."

The waitress came back with the tea and asked, "Anything else?"

"Just the check, please," Aron said and then turned to me. "Jack, you have the cards you are dealt with in life. It's up to you to play those cards the best that you can to get other cards."

The bill came and Aron insisted on picking it up. I felt like I had found my surrogate grandparents in New York. Aron and Maja reminded me of the couples I saw dining in the Munich restaurant in Rio de Janeiro, and even of Clayton Black, the World War II photographer I met in Chicago.

"Thank you, Aron," I said as he signed the credit card receipt. "Of course, Jack."

"I'd love to do this again," I said.

"Yes, that would be nice," Maja responded. "Why don't you come over to our house for brunch one of these weekends?"

"How about next Sunday?"

"That works just fine," Aron said.

"Here is our address," Maja handed me a paper napkin with their address on it. "Come by around ten."

"Great! I look forward to it."

We got up from the table and walked outside the restaurant, where a number of students were smoking Parliaments and socializing. A crisp spring breeze came in from the Hudson River and brushed our faces. I buttoned my jean jacket over my white t-shirt and threw my messenger bag over my shoulder. Aron and Maja bundled up for their Vepsa ride back to their apartment on the Upper West Side. I shook Aron's hand and kissed Maja twice – once on each cheek.

"See you Sunday, Jack," Maja said with a warm smile.

"See you Sunday," I responded with the smile you have when you arrive at your destination after a long journey and feel relieved that you got there somehow.

CHAPTER 33

Sometimes, Heroes Are Dodgy

I awoke the following Sunday morning and headed up to Aron and Maja's apartment on the Upper West Side. The sun was shining. It was the start of springtime. The air was cool, but not cold. When I walked into the apartment building, it felt ancient. As I walked under dim lights in the entryway, the brightness of the sun faded. Gargoyle designs plastered the walls of the library-quiet hallway.

"Maja and Aron, please."

"Yes," the doorman said. "They are expecting you. Take the elevator over there to the penthouse floor."

"Thank you, sir."

"You are welcome," the doorman nodded and closed the gate behind me as I entered the old school elevator. I stood silently as it took me to the top floor.

When I exited, I was greeted by Aron's warm voice:

"Welcome, Jack, welcome!"

Aron smiled and shook my hand with his trademark firm grip. He was wearing a Cannondale bicycle outfit – tight shorts, nylon top, and shoes that clamp into the pedals.

"This is something for you and Maja," I said handing him the bottle of wine that I had picked up from the local store,

"You didn't need to, Jack."

"I wanted to."

"Come, come inside." He softly put his hand on my back and guided me inside.

The bright sun shone through the massive windows onto everything in the 20-foot high ceiling apartment – the brown bison Chesterfield sofa, the Modigliani artwork, and the black Steinway piano. There was a small balcony outside on which the Bethes had a table, chairs, and an umbrella for entertaining. Jazz was playing on their Bose stereo. I believe it was "Take Five" by Dave Brubeck.

"Jack, welcome to our home." Maja came out of the kitchen smiling warmly. She was wearing a white linen tunic to her knees, a silver Cartier tank Francaise watch, different colored bracelets (blue, green, red), and red espadrilles.

I gave her a warm hug. "Thank you Maja. Your apartment is so pretty. So very pretty." As Maja and I broke off our hug, she looked me in the eyes:

"Thank you, Jack, we love it. And we love sharing it with people like you. So come on through and eat some of this dew." She handed me a plate of honeydew. I couldn't wait. "Come, come sit down," she said. We walked over to a large brown oak country table. Sunflowers were in a vase in the middle of the table.

After I sat down, she asked: "Can I get you anything to drink?"

"Water please."

"Of course. Sparkling?"

"Yes, please," I nodded.

Maja went to the kitchen to get the water. I looked towards the outside balcony and saw a splendid spread of fresh bagels, lox, orange juice, coffee, and fresh fruit on the table underneath the cover of the umbrella.

"What a wonderful spread, Maja," I said looking at her in the kitchen, which was outfitted with a Wolf stove, an industrial-size Sub Zero fridge, and a large black granite island. "You guys didn't need to put yourselves out like this for me."

"It is our pleasure," Maja said, as she handed me a bottle of Pellegrino sparkling water. "Where is Aron?"

"He went to take a shower. He just came back from a bike ride in the park," she pointed out towards the park, "and then he is going to prepare some of the sweets for after we eat." I looked toward the park below and saw its trees. They looked like bunches of fresh broccoli that were slightly visible over the relatively short balcony concrete wall. I took a sip of the water and then asked:

"How long have you guys been living here?"

"For several years. We bought it back in 1980s," Maja said.

We went to sit down at the Crate and Barrel brown summer table outside. As we ate, I asked Maja:

"I have been meaning to ask you, Maja, but I never had the chance. How did you escape?"

Maja picked up her coffee, sipped it, put it back down, and then looked at me: "My mother and I were smuggled to the Italian occupied territories in 1941." She paused.

"By whom?" I asked.

"With the help of complete strangers," she looked at me.

I digested that for a second. I thought about my mother's family in France and how many were part of the Resistance, especially in Lyon and Marseille. Resistance members from the mountains, she told me once, were called the *Maquis,* the name of a Corsican black bird. According to my research, some members in the Resistance were dodgy – one I read about was a chain smoking janitor. I wondered if, maybe, one of my ancestors in the Resistance helped Maja and her family.

"They risked their lives to save you even though they didn't know you?" I asked with surprise.

"Yes."

She paused again, looked out towards the park, and then continued: "And it wasn't who you might expect," she said.

"What do you mean?" I took a big sip of my coffee.

"A lot of the resistance movements in countries like France weren't made up of the 'crème of the crop.'"

"You mean they weren't the bourgeois?"

"Precisely," she nodded. "Most of the bourgeois had too much to lose. A lot of them became complacent during the war. Instead of fighting or resisting, many of them just chose to cooperate. That way, they wouldn't lose what they had."

She sipped her coffee and took a big bite of her bagel. "Like in Vichy?" I asked.

Vichy was the headquarters of occupied France.

"Like in Vichy. The Vichy French not only cooperated with, but actually actively assisted, the Nazis," she said to me with a killer look in her eyes.

She paused to look at the park.

"What's the difference?" I asked with a shrug. "The result is the same." She turned her attention back to me:

"There is a difference between sitting by while others do something you should say something about and actively assisting them. The Vichy French government actively assisted," she said as she wagged her right index finger.

"So then who made up the Resistance? Who helped you the most?" I bit into my bagel as a breeze from Central Park caused all of the blooming greenery on her balcony to sway.

Maja took a bite of her bagel and looked out into the park. She then turned to me: "You may be surprised, but it was regular people and even some irregular people."

"Like?" I asked.

"There were the farmers, blue-collar factory workers, and the dockworkers. But then you also had bootleggers and unsavory types who pitched into the cause as well."

"Don't get me wrong," she continued after taking a sip of her coffee. "It wasn't that there weren't any bourgeois people in on it. It's just that most clung onto their . . ."

"Possessions?" I interrupted.

"Those," she nodded, "and also onto their safety. There are many of that ilk who actually lived very comfortable lifestyles."

"Even during the war?" I asked in disbelief.

"Even during the war," she said as she sat back in her chair to take in the scene. "And so while the Nazis were rounding up people, the collaborators would eat caviar, go to plays, drink champagne, and basically live a life that was not much different from the life they lived before the war."

"I imagine these people thought," I looked up into the sky ever so briefly and then back at Maja, "'why should I risk everything for a Jew?'"

"Or a gypsy, or even a Christian," Maja said with a smile. "What do you mean?" I asked curiously.

Maja finished the bite of her bagel.

"Jews weren't the only targets of Hitler's ire. Those others were targets, too."

"So why did the other folks you mentioned fight? What was in it for them? I mean, how did they stand to profit from participating in the Resistance?"

I took a large gulp of my orange juice.

"Good question," Maja said as she moved forward in her chair. "The only way I can answer it is by reflecting on how they say pedophiles and rapists in jail have to worry about being murdered by the bank robbers or drug-running bikers."

"Meaning?" I asked with a raised eyebrow.

"Oftentimes, there is a code even among those who don't seem to have a code," she paused to see if I was following her, "and so the bank robber doesn't have a problem stealing from a large, wealthy bank. But he might have a problem seeing innocent children placed into ovens."

"And what about the others?" I took a sip of my coffee.

"Very simply, there are some people who stand up, and there are others who don't. Perhaps for some in the bourgeois, there was pressure to cooperate so as to keep up appearances." She took a big sip of her coffee, a bite of her watermelon, and then continued:

"Many people can't handle the thought of not having their favorite car, their butler, or whatever else they have that gives them safety, you see. It is part of their identity and reputation. So, for many of these people, I imagine they would have felt dead without their badges of elitism."

I looked around Maja's immaculate apartment. I imagined how different their living must have been when they were in the rat hole that measured 350 square feet, with one bedroom, cockroach problems, collapsing roof when it rained too much, and no doorman to greet guests. They have done without before, and now they lived in splendor. But I didn't doubt that they would have given it all up if keeping it meant being complicit with a government like Vichy.

"And yet, it seems to me, it was the ones who fought who were the elite," I concluded. "Yes," Maja nodded to me, "but the Resistance fighters were considered criminals at that time by the Vichy regime." She sipped her coffee in a matter of fact way. "So it was very un-

bourgeois to be a part of the Resistance, regardless of what country you are talking about, because it was . . . "

" A faux pas to be a criminal?"

"You could say that," Maja agreed.

"And so many sheep just fell into line?"

I put my hand on the table to indicate a procession. "Precisely. It was mostly the outliers who resisted."

"The oddballs?"

"In a way, yes."

"Well," I sipped my coffee, "I guess it is mostly the outliers who make serious advances in society. Look at Einstein!"

"Yea, he was pretty ugly!" she smiled.

"He wasn't exactly a J. Crew model. Every day, he wore a black suit, white shirt, and black tie. I understand he invited a black lady friend of his to Princeton when the school was rampant with racism and anti-Semitism. Not that I have anything against J. Crew per se. I mean, my shorts are from J. Crew."

I pointed at my seersucker shorts, and we smiled playfully at one another.

"They say that, to be a good leader, Jack, you can't walk in the herd of sheep. Like Aron said earlier, sometimes you have to leave the herd to take the best path. That requires you to be alone, or at least not surrounded by the rest of the herd. Many people are afraid of doing that."

She cut some cantaloupe on the table.

"I think he is right, Maja. If you are in a herd of sheep, you kind of follow the sheep in front of you, on the side of you, and even those behind you. You are so worried about what other sheep think about you that you fail to think about what is or should be important to you. You go with the flow of the herd. The herd turns right, you turn right, or if the herd turns left, you turn left, without even seeing what is in front," I said.

"You trust the herd, and particularly the sheep in the front of the herd, to steer you the right way," Maja said. "You follow the herd because you think they will protect you. Their interests are supposed to be your own. Some of this makes sense. I mean, sometimes its better to be in a crowd, like if you are meeting a potentially dangerous person. But, in other cases, you are making yourself more vulnerable to attack."

"An easy target?" I cut some cantaloupe, too.

"It's harder to hit a bunch of sheep spread across the world than a bunch of sheep concentrated in one island, like Manhattan," she said as she pointed to the surrounding city.

"But maybe the herd's interests are in fact your own?"

"Of course. Maybe being with the herd will allow you to live the life you want during war – drinking what you want, eating what you want, being where you want, and the like.

"Like the French in Vichy?"

"Like the French in Vichy," she said. "Want some more coffee, Jack?"

"Yes, please."

As she poured the coffee, Maja continued:

"But perhaps you lose sight of what the herd is doing to provide you with these niceties because you are so caught in the middle of the herd that you lose sight of its place in relation to other herds. To the top?" she asked.

"Yes, please. Fill it up."

She finished filling my mug.

"At the same time, Jack, if you are too much of a wolf and walk too far in front of the herd, then the sheep will not follow you."

"Why?" I sipped some of the French roast.

"They will be afraid of you. You aren't part of the herd." She smiled wryly as her hand shook taking the coffee to her mouth.

"A dangerous outsider?"

"Precisely," she slowly placed the coffee back on the table. "They won't follow an outsider unless the outsider builds credibility. This usually means being close enough to the group to ensure they realize that the outsider's interests are roughly the same as theirs."

The music from the inside at this point had changed from Dave Brubeck to Chopin's "Ballade No. 4 in F Minor."

"But not identical?" I asked.

"Can't be identical," she nodded her head, "otherwise, there is no way for the leader to lead. A real leader, in a way, has to be somewhat of an outsider, in order to do things that other people want or wish or desire to do, but don't have the courage to do."

"Or perhaps, initially, they don't even want what the leader says they should want," I said looking over at the park. "Maybe they change their minds later on because the leader is able to convince them to change their ways," I said looking back at Maja.

"So the leader is both the outsider and the insider, in a way," Maja concluded.

"That's a tough balance to achieve." I looked at her in disbelief. It's as though she just said a leader should be able to walk on shark-infested waters while coolly smoking a cigarette and balancing a cup of English tea in one hand.

"It's an art, not a science," Maja said seriously. "Some leaders don't ever convince the herd to change their ways. Look at Copernicus. He was considered a heretic by the sheep. They never accepted his thoughts . . ."

"Until after he was dead," I interrupted. "But, by then, it was too late for him." I tried to think of a leader that had a good ending.

"That is but one example among so many," Maja said. She paused and I grew excited to hear her next example. "Hitler was actually an outsider," she said.

I looked at her with my mouth slightly agape. He wasn't what I was looking for.

"He wasn't from German aristocracy. He wasn't even German – Austrian actually. But he lit a fire on the brush that was German pain from World War I, and the German people's hatred of their economic situation. He gave the German people something to believe in, someone to blame it on, and a clear solution to their problems."

"The Final Solution?" I asked.

"Or, in German, 'Die Endlösung,'" she astutely pointed out.

"It seemed like that was, for the German people at the time, a quick antidepressant," acting as if I were putting a pill in my mouth. "They could take the pill in lieu of going through therapy, or of doing the heavy lifting necessary to see what their problem was."

I took a bite of my cantaloupe.

"Yes," Maja agreed. "The Germans escaped into the Final Solution, thinking it would be their quick fix, only to find out <u>it actually made things worse</u>."

"It seems like an easy trap to fall into," I said. "The mirage is that the next drink or hit will give you peace," I said and paused. "But the next drink or hit only brings you farther and farther away from the solution." I looked down onto the table with a slightly despondent look. I wondered if my life fit that description precisely. I looked up at her and she smiled at me.

"There is no question it is an easy trap." She put her hand down flat on the table to get my attention. I smiled.

The music playing now in the background was "My Way" by Frank Sinatra.

"I get it." I put my hand on my chin. "The barriers for outsiders to enter the media market were higher before. Now things happen almost instantaneously. When something happens in Cairo, you see it on the web almost when it happens."

"Completely," Maja said nodding in agreement. "It's as if the speed of sound and light are one."

"It's so odd." I took a sip of the coffee, put it down, and then continued. "Events like the Holocaust are revolting to think about. I can't believe human beings are capable of such things. And yet I can't believe that these people in the Resistance were often . . . "

"Misfits?" Maja said. "Right," I leaned forward.

"What happened to your father?" I asked.

She looked off into the park, paused, and then looked at me sadly. "He died when I was two years old."

"Did you stay in Italy?"

"Yes. In 1943, after the Croatians and the Allied Forces toppled the Fascists, my mother and I fled to what is now Santa Bianca al Bagno in southern Italy, where we stayed until the end of WWII."

"Did you ever go back to Sarajevo?"

"In 1945 we did. But we left Communist Yugoslavia and settled in Israel in about 1948."

"It must have been tough for you and your family."

"It was. We were horribly poor. We had nothing. I never want to be poor again."

"When did you go into the Israeli military?"

"About 1959."

"And that is where you met Aron, as I recall."

"Yes."

"And you stayed in Israel?"

"We left after the Six-Day-War in 1967. Aron, our daughter and I moved to Paris, where Aron earned his doctorate and I earned a degree in philosophy. I later pursued a doctorate."

"When did you all come to the States?"

"In about 1972. I have always said that this country gave us a chance to rise as far as we could imagine."

"I think you mentioned you got your doctorate. When did you have time for that?"

"At the apex of my business career in the jewelry business, I left to go back to school."

"Inspiring! I wanted to ask you something specific about the camps, but I don't want to drag down the day," I said as I put the utensils on the plate and started to bring things closer to bring them into the kitchen.

"Don't worry about all of that, Jack. I'll take care of it," she said with a smile. "Are you sure?"

"Yes," she nodded.

As I said this, Aron came out to join us wearing a white linen shirt, white linen pants, brown leather sandals, his Panerai watch, and Ray Ban pilot sunglasses. It was about 11:30 a.m. The sun was shining brightly above.

The song "Goin' to Chicago" by jazz great Joe Williams was now playing on the stereo. Maja responded:

"You won't drag it down, Jack. I am still alive, but I won't be alive for much longer. So while I am around, I feel that I need to tell others what happened."

Maja took a bite from her watermelon.

Aron looked at me intensely but then cracked a smile. He put his napkin on his lap, started picking up some of the lox, cream cheese, and bagels, and then chimed in:

"She is right. People like us will not be around forever, Jack. So it is good for us to be able to tell others, in other generations, what happened."

"In that case, Maja," I clasped my hands together in front of me on the table out of nervousness. "My question is: did you ever ask your mom what the Nazis did to exterminate everyone so efficiently?"

"Yes. And I know from others what they did."

She stopped eating, sat back in her chair, wiped her mouth with the napkin, and gazed briefly down into Central Park. She then looked at me with an intense stare, without blinking, like the one Frank gave me the night when he came to pick me up in Venice Beach. She explained the routine the Nazis used to pass people through the showers. She then took a sip out of her coffee mug and kept her finely manicured hands around it as Aron stopped eating to slowly rub her shoulder.

I observed:

"I don't know if my generation knows of such pain, Maja."

"Previous generations fought so others would not have to. Instead, the newer generations, like yours," she held out her palm towards me, "can innovate. I mean, look at all of the Internet applications and advances that have been made."

"I guess that is true," I said, unsure of my statement.

"And yet I agree with you!" she said. "You remember when we went to dinner that night with Aron, right?"

"Yes."

"Remember when we talked about instant gratification?"

"Yes."

"In a way, I think many in your generation have that instant gratification mentality because they have not had to persevere over severe adversity."

"But I have gathered from speaking to both of you," I said, "that to keep acting courageously requires perseverance over the persistent fear that arises."

A small breeze passed softly over our faces.

"A persistent fear that can arise every day, Jack," Aron said. "These fears can be a fear of failure, a fear of death, a fear of loss, or a fear of initially. Some people encounter these fears when they wake up in the morning. And that is why it is important to be vigilant in facing these fears, to understand them, and to persevere over them."

"Winning the battle today is necessary but not sufficient for winning the war?" I asked. "The war is a life long process."

Aron then stopped eating his bagel and commented further:

"At the same time, perseverance requires something many people often undervalue and are too self-righteous to exercise," Aron said to me with a small smirk. He paused and looked at me.

I waited for him to continue. Then he said:

"This is your cue, Jack, to ask me 'what?'"

I sipped my coffee, wiped my face, and put my napkin down: "Sorry, Aron. Here it goes . . ."

"Should I prepare a drum roll?" Aron said as he did a mock drum roll on the table with his index fingers. "Or, better yet, did you stretch before you came here? I mean, I don't want you to hurt your mouth when exerting the effort entailed in such an enterprise!"

We smiled at one another. "Here I go: what?"

Then Aron cogently said:

"Humor."

"Humor?" I asked with surprise.

"Right, humor," Aron nodded. "Without a sense of humor, life is heavy, dark, and full of never-ending suffering. Humor is a shock absorber that takes on the events of life that would otherwise break us. And when I say 'humor,' I don't mean that everything is funny. That is a form of denial."

"So what do you mean then?" I asked.

"I mean that it is oftentimes healthy to laugh at the absurdity of life with others. It is also healthy to laugh at yourself when you make mistakes, assuming you have first learned from them."

"Otherwise, you get too uptight?" I asked.

"Right," he nodded. "Having a good sense of humor alleviates the pressure inside us and is a gift from God . . . "

"Or whatever it is that is out there." I pointed around us in reference to the ambiguity of God being some old man with a beard or actually a spirit in the universe.

"Or maybe he or it is in there," he said pointing to the black coffee in front of him with a sarcastic smirk, "or maybe there;" he pointed to the fly on the table.

Bob Dylan's song, "Visions of Johanna," was now playing in the background.

"Whatever it is you want to call it, or wherever it is. Words, to me, are incapable of referring to something if you don't even know what it is you are trying to refer to," he concluded.

"Meaning?" I asked.

"The word 'rose' gives me an image of a flower and a smell in my head. But I wouldn't have that image unless I had first seen and smelled a flower. The same is true here."

"As with 'rose,' I wouldn't know what 'humor' meant unless I had experienced laughter."

He nodded.

"Now, you are getting the picture, Jack?" he said with inquiring eyes and raised eyebrows.

CHAPTER 34

Turn On, Tune In, But Don't Drop Out

My memories of Aron and Maja faded when the *Kind of Blue* album I was listening to in my apartment ended. It was about 6:30 p.m. I wasn't ready to go to bed just yet, so I fixed a quick meal of pasta, fresh garlic, and tomatoes. After the meal, I put on the album *Rockin' Steady* by Desmond Decker, the Jamaican recording artist. As the song "Wise Man" came on, I sipped some Malbec and Ace appeared in my head.

Ace was sitting on a black, wooden Quaker chair in the middle of the beach in Cefalu, Sicily. It was about 1:00 in the morning. The ocean waves crashed ever so slightly in the background. His two black Labradors were at his side. Their heads were resting softly on the sand.

"So are you getting the picture, Jack?" Ace asked looking at me through his Harry Potter like clear frames. "You have to practice staying turning on, tuning in, and not dropping out, cause your date may want to make out." Ace's tuxedo pants were rolled up above his crossed legs. I briefly glanced at his Casper-white, bare feet. He was smoking a light cigar. He was sitting with Maja and Aron, who were also dressed elegantly but with bare feet, too. They were all seated in the Quaker chairs and were enjoying the Sicilian sky. It was a violet and blue tapestry of small and large stars whose ancient light had traveled light years before it reached our petite planet.

"I think so," I answered. I was standing in front of them. Maja and Aron looked intently into my eyes. "I am getting clearer on the perseverance thing. I mean, I get how you need to face your demons, whatever they are, every day. I guess there aren't any easy outs. But I am not clear about humor. I mean, how can someone be humorous without being in denial? Isn't humor just as much of an escape as any other addiction?"

"Remember the puppeteer you met on Pirate's Alley?" Ace asked me. "The one who had cancer and had just left the hospital?" I said.

"That one," he said as he took off his glasses and looked deeply at me.

So as I lay there on my couch, I thought back to the puppeteer with cancer I had met in Pirate's Alley, New Orleans. I was 33 years old when I traveled there for a business trip a few months after meeting Maja and Aaron.

(G) HUMOR

CHAPTER 35

I Love Playing Russian Roulette

"While I waz doing my act in Iraq, I see zat ze juggler had a number of starz on his ballz, you know, but, em, not ze ones between your legs."

The puppeteer, who said his name was Enzo, paused, looked up at me from his wheel chair, and grinned. I thought he was nuts! I stumbled upon the puppeteer speaking to his audience as I was walking down the Alley one steaming and humid night.

"One of the guards saw, too, and thought ze juggler was a Jewish spy. So he slice de man into two. I could not believe zis!"

Enzo put his hands up in a touchdown position and looked to the sky to indicate his disbelief.

"But I have lot of fun in Iraq during ziz times," he said as he put his hands down. "I mean, I love playing Russian roulette, but juggling in Iraq was much better, eh?"

He laughed a mad laugh, "ah, ah, ah, ah, ah, ah," as he slapped his knee.

"I remember how Saddam had a number of swords from former conquests that he kept on hand.

Like a collection of skulls, he kept them to show others," he told me as he looked at the flow of people walking through Pirate's Alley.

"Wow, you have really been around," I said as I stared down at him, "what is your full name?"

He looked up at me from his wheelchair holding his hand out.

"Enzo Perrier Bonaparte," he said looking up to me as we shook hands.

The blue blooded named puppeteer and I were sitting and standing, respectively, in Pirate's Alley. It was originally named Ruelle d'Orleans, and its current distressed cobblestones were laid around 1831. The Alley connects Jackson Square with Royal Street, is about 16 feet wide and 600 feet long, and runs past the Creole house that housed William Faulkner when he wrote *Soldier's Pay* in 1926. Ferns and flowers usually hang from the balconies of the Creole houses that line the Alley. Legend has it that Andrew Jackson met with Jean Lafitte, the raffish, but ruthlessly creative, French-born privateer and pirate, in the Alley. During the meeting, Jackson asked Lafitte whether he would assist him against the Spanish during the pending battle of New Orleans. Lafitte did just that.

Like Lafitte before him, the raffish puppeteer's face was unwashed and worn from exposure to the sun. His small, squinty eyes were full of fun. Draping down on his shoulders were his thinning black strands of hair. Protruding outwards from under his nose was a large, untrimmed, bushy mustache that slightly went around his lips. He took trips through the crowds of onlookers and hookers in the French

Quarter by pushing himself in a wheelchair with opened fingered gloves on his hands. While his spirit was free, he looked like he was in the grips of death: pants torn at the knees, white unwashed collared shirt showing his gray chest hair, and feeble arms and legs like those of a malnourished, five-year-old boy.

"Alors, ladies and gentlemen, ziz are my two bonnes amis, Louis and Edith." ("Bonnes amis" is good friends in French.) He then bowed, introduced himself as Enzo, and caused his two puppets to bow, too.

When I heard Enzo's accent, I stopped to listen and watch him play with his two charming puppets.

Enzo's male puppet was named Louis, a roughly 60-year-old, dapper black man with a saxophone. Louis wore a straw hat, a mustache that was going gray, a similarly colored trimmed Afro under a brown straw fedora, a brown bow tie, a brown, double-breasted, chalk-stripe suit, and white and brown spectator shoes that you would see at the Kentucky Derby. Of course, the trumpeter puppet had a handkerchief. He was a dapper New Orleans gent.

Next to Louis was the puppet named Edith. She looked about 50 with large breasts and a rotund behind that pushed itself outside the sides of her black hip hugging pencil skirt dress. Her sugar white skin was framed by blond hair down to her shoulders. She wore red heels, a tomato red blouse that exposed her chest, and little gold earnings that accentuated her strawberry colored lips.

I waited for the puppeteer to finish his act, and then I walked over to him: "Tu parles Francais?" I asked him. (Do you speak French?)

"Oui," he answered. (Yes.)

"Ma mere est Francaise," I explained. (My mother is French.)

Enzo paused as he sat on his wheelchair to watch the flow of people walking through Pirate's alley. There were hippy kids from Rollins College who wore dirty hemp bracelets and t- shorts from Widespread Panic; Japanese kids who shop at Supreme, the store in New York, wearing X Large brand backpacks and taking photos of the Alley; proper looking Southern Christian couples from places like Baton Rouge, Alexandria, and Huntsville; and sloppy-drunk business people who were likely in town for a dental conference.

As Enzo watched the people walk by, he commented to me:

"I am zo happy to be out here," and then he looked up at me contently.

Initially, I could not really agree with him. Steam rose off the alcohol and urine-soaked cobble stone street. My white t-shirt was drenched with sweat while my hair looked as though I just came out an olive oil shower. But my anxious thoughts that day were thankfully interrupted:

"I just got out of ze hospital," Enzo said as he looked back towards the morass of people. "I waz alone in ze room. There waz a television above my bed," as he motioned with his hand upward, "I lay in ze bed -- all day. I lay in bed -- all ze night. I could not move. The cancer – it eats my body, comme une hamburger. (Like a hamburger.) Parts of my body are rotten, comme une purri pomme. (Like a rotten apple.) And the chemo paralyze my legs, so I have to be in zis chair for very long time now." He hit the wheelchair with his right hand. "But I zinc in a way zat dis is way for God to speak to me, a way for me to be closer to Him, and my way of doing ziz is to make people laugh, eh?"

As I listened to the Enzo, I looked at his wrinkled hands. They had received too much chemotherapy – or perhaps not enough. On his left hand, he had a pinky ring fitted with an aqua blue stone. On the other, a tarnished, vintage Cartier tank watch.

"Where are you from?" I asked Enzo.

"Corsica," he answered. "But I have been all over the world – I have lived in New Orleans for some time. Before that, I was in Iraq, France, and Italy."

That is when he told me about his juggling for Saddam.

"Should you be out here? It looks like you are still recovering," I asked him with concern, even though I knew the concern was somewhat wasted breath, like it would have been with my father. Enzo, like my pop, was going to do as he pleased, come hell or high water. The difference being that Enzo was pleasant, not acidic, and was accepting of death, not in denial of it.

"Mon ami, ziz iz my recovery!" He looked up at me with a stare that said: you have no idea what you are talking about.

"Huh?"

That's when I learned from Enzo more about what Aron had told me about humor and its place in coping with the curveballs that life throws us.

CHAPTER 36

Laughter: Cheaper Than A Massage

"Listen to me, mon ami. I couldn't stand being in ze hospital, trapped by ze mindless babble on the television, ze Brittany Spears ziz, ze Brittany Spears zat, ze four wallz of ze room, and all of zeez sick people," he looked towards the filthy ground to indicate his dislike of the hospital.

"You see, mon ami," he reached up to pat me softly on my shoulder, "laughter is what we must do to water ze tree zat is our soul. Without laughter, without ze lightness zat you get from zeeing yourself and others smile and smirk, you might az well be dead. Laughter iz meditation. It brings you a, how you say, fresh mind," he used his index finger to tap his temple, "to ze same zings you zee every day, incest, adultery, jealousy, and, for me, cancer, you see?"

Enzo looked me straight in the eye, like a father does his son, to make sure I got the point. It was the same straight eye that Frank gave me that night and the same one that Maja gave me that time during morning brunch. It was a deadly serious look.

"I take my chemotherapy and medication. But I don't stay in the ze hospital because ziz is my energy," he pointed to the strangers walking by on the alley. "You see? My audience givez me ze energie to see to ze next day."

"Capisco." I gladly told him. The puppeteer then winked at me.

"Very well, mon ami, I must move on and get to my laughter medicine."

"I understand," I nodded.

"But before I do, I have a joke for you."

"A joke?" I asked surprised.

"Mais, of course. And you don't even need health insurance," he said with a wry smile. "Alright," I said, "let's hear it."

"So there is ziz man in New York City," he looked up at me. "Ok."

"He live in a apartment, uh, you know, on ze second floor of apartment. Zere is ziz woman who lives above him," he pointed up with his right index finger. "She has glass eye. Ze man and ze woman want to know if it is raining."

"Ok."

"So in the morning both put zere heads out of zere windowz and put their palms out." He put his palm outwards. "All of a sudden, ze woman's glass eye falls out. Guess what happens?"

"What?"

"It drops, ploop, in ze man's palm." Enzo looks down into his palm.

"So ze man looks at his palm, and says 'Oh shit, she lost her eye!' Ze man goes upstairs and knocks on woman's door. 'Knock, knock, knock,'" Enzo knocks on his wheelchair.. "Ze woman answers and ze man holds her glass eye out in his hand." Enzo holds his palm out.

"She says, 'Oh, zank you, zank you, zank you so very much. Please come in, I have food to give you, coffee, donuts, and sweets.' So ze man come into the apartment, and ze woman give de man many nice things."

"Ze man sits with her for an hour or so and asks ze woman, 'Do you give zo many nice zings like this to all of ze men zat come into your apartment?'"

"Ze woman looks at him, very carefully, and says: 'Non, only ze ones dat catch my eye!'"

Enzo and I both giggled like two little schoolgirls. "Bonne soiree," he said, a French good night.

"Et bonne soiree, monsieur."

CHAPTER 37

Pink Kelly Bag

"You see, Jack," Ace interjected into my thoughts, "humor isn't necessarily denial or escape," he said as he sat on the beach in Cefalu. Ace was not in his trademark Victorian Gothic looking tuxedo.

He was cross-dressed in a Southern woman's outfit of a seersucker jacket and white linen blouse, skirt, pearl necklace, black and white Ferragamo spectator pumps, pink lipstick, Cartier earrings, and a pink Hermes Kelly bag.

"What?" I said to him.

He was still wearing his white gold signet ring, but he had on light nail polish that matched the color of his pink Kelly bag. He looked like a preppy, Southern, Episcopal version of the characters played by Tony Curtis and Jack Lemmon in the 1959 movie *Some Like It Hot*.

"What the hell?" I said again to him.

"The use of humor certainly shows weakness!" I said in frustration to Ace. I pictured myself gripping the Sicilian sand underneath my bare feet. "I mean, look at yourself and the way you are dressed! It is funny, no doubt," I said with a condescending chuckle. "But you look like a fucking sissy. I mean, the puppeteer was funny, but he was kind of weak. And it looks like you are, too," I said frustrated.

"I could see your simpleton part of your mind at work. That's why I wore this classy outfit," Ace replied in his calm tone, "one that used to look smashing on a woman named Sophia I used to know back in New York City, but which looks absurd on me," he said looking at himself.

"So you put that on to make a point?" I wondered.

He paused. I imagine the waves crashing in the background.

"Chew on this, sonny," Ace said to me. "At the end of 2008, about four men stole about

$108 million in jewels from Harry Winston in Paris. It was the biggest jewelry heist in French history."

"Yea, big deal." I said.

"Two of the men were cross-dressed as classy Sophia Gordon looking women. Their partners were dressed as classy men."

"Really?"

"Really," Ace said. "You see, Jack, just because someone has a sense of humor, which these men certainly did, it doesn't mean they are weak. These men played their outfits to their advantage. It camouflaged their strength."

I paused. And then I realized the method to his apparent madness. "I get it. You are a counterexample?" I asked.

"I am. But I think the puppeteer was a sufficient counterexample. He was your pink Kelly bag, figuratively speaking."

"How?" I asked.

"How many people in his condition did you see out on the streets of New Orleans telling jokes, playing with puppets, and so on?"

"None."

"Exceptional person then?"

"Yes," I nodded.

"Why?" Ace asked.

"Because he was using his sense of humor to help him persevere over his cancer. He wasn't merely submitting to it."

"Do you think he was angry at his cancer?" Ace asked. "I would think so," I shrugged.

"And yet he was out there on the street, hustling."

"Right."

"With the faith that getting out of the hospital fishbowl would help him, not hurt him?"

"Well, yes. I mean, he hadn't done it before, so there was a leap there."

"An escape?"

"Yes, but a healthy one."

"And do you think he needed to smoke a joint before he went out on the street?"

"I doubt it."

"Why?"

I imagined a larger wave crashing in the background.

"Because he seemed so high on life. He was ecstatic about being out there – breathing, seeing, feeling, loving, smiling, speaking, smelling, sweating, thinking, creating. I think he appreciated every moment he was out there."

"And so you see," Ace said as he looked into my eyes. "Humor doesn't make such a man a weak sissy, just like this pink Kelly bag doesn't make me a force not to be reckoned with," he said with a playful grin. "Most people think that a man needs to be stoic at such times, not

showing any emotion, being 'strong,' like some statute.Otherwise, if he cries, or shows his feelings, the majority of people would likely consider him not to be a 'true' man."

I thought about that for a second as I lay there in my apartment.

"It seems the emotional man is stronger than the emotionless man. It's like he is embracing his mortality with his eyes wide open," I said.

Ace responded:

"The emotionless man needs the pistol by his side because anger is his emotion. But that plug also keeps him shut off from loss, love, and pleasure, Jack."

The next thing I knew, Ace had changed from his classy, Southern woman outfit. He was back in his three-piece tuxedo with the gothic, Victorian, silver-plated pocket watch dangling from his vest pocket. We were back in the library in Chicago. Ace's legs were crossed as he sat on the Chesterfield couch petting Lila and Duke.

"Don't be ashamed about having a sense of humor, Jack. Use it in your life. It's a badge of courage, not a badge of weakness."

At that point, I opened my eyes. It was almost 11:30 p.m. I had an early morning appointment with my accountant Arthur Rubin the next morning. I was looking forward to going over my taxes with him. I cleaned the dishes, put them away, brushed my teeth, and went to lie down on my bed.

PART III
AWAKENING

CHAPTER 38

Nightmare Catch 22

"How does the defendant plead?" The judge asked.

As I sat in a squad car on the way to the Los Angeles County Men's Central Jail, I knew there would be one of two answers to the judge's question. A few days after Frank, Butch, and Paula picked me up from the Venice Beach party, I was charged by the Los Angeles district attorney's office with nine counts of first-degree murder under California Penal Code Section 187. In California, as in most states, an accomplice to a murder is as culpable as the murderer. I was considered an accomplice because I was the pointer for Frank and Mick. I knew where the boys hung out. Frank and Mick did the rest, along with Paula. Under the statute, I was due to either spend the rest of my life in prison or receive the death penalty.

"You are in a catch-22," my attorney, Mel Hyman said when he came to see me in the holding cell.

Mel's family had been representing major organized crime figures around the country, including

San Francisco, New York, and Chicago, since at least the early 1800s. Like my father, Mel had moved to Los Angeles from New York City as a youth. Mel grew up in Echo Park, fought in World War II, and attended Columbia Law. He was about five foot five and a savvy trial lawyer who had represented some of the biggest crime figures in the country. He had a hooked nose, manicured nails, a receding gray hairline, and bags under his eyes. His crouched back made him "the hunch back from The Bronx." He always sported a slick Brioni suit, grey Brioni tie and crisp Brioni white shirt, simple silver rectangular cuff links, bench-made English loafers, and a white gold pinky ring with a black onyx inset. When he left his office in Century City or his home in Beverly Hills, it was always in his Maserati Quattroporte IV. Farid, a six- foot-six menacing looking Algerian, was Mel's driver. The investigative staff at his law firm included elite former CIA agents.

"Assume you plead not guilty," Mel said as he leaned forward over the table and looked me dead in the eyes.

"Damn right!" I slammed my fist onto the table. "We fight it! We damage the credibility of their witness, right?" I said with a glimmer of hope.

"Yea, yea, I get it, son." He sat back in his chair and waved my idea away with his right hand like it was an annoying fly. "The problem with your idea is that they have excellent witnesses. They are clean cut, have no records, and have no motive to lie. We may be able to call into question their ability to identify you late at night like that, but it's a big gamble.

So think about this: we go to trial, you lose, and then what?"

"I'm fucked?" I said with my eyebrows raised.

"Yea, you got that right, young man," Mel said in his thick fatherly Bronx accent. "You'll go to prison – for a long time – or get the death penalty. But, if you play ball, I think I can pull strings to get you out of this pretty smoothly."

"How much time would I do if we lost at trial?" I asked.

"At least 25 to life, and likely somewhere like Folsom," he looked at me with somberly. "And what about afterwards, if there is an afterwards. What would become of me?" I asked with a fearful tremble in my voice.

"Are you serious, Jack?" he asked with a crooked grin. "Yes," I nodded earnestly.

"If you get out, you will be more or less unemployable with felonies like this on your record." He leaned forward in his chair and put his elbows on the table. "So, after working at some dead end jobs for a time, you'll probably go into some illicit trade as a low level operator. You are too ambitious to work at Taco Hell for long."

We both paused and looked at one another in silence for a few seconds. "Drug game?" I broke the silence.

"Maybe, but maybe something else," Mel said with a slight shrug to his shoulders, "like sophisticated arms."

"Would I stay there, I mean, at the lower level?" I asked in a fearful, anxiety-ridden voice. I knew Mel would know. He knew the game very well.

"You are ambitious," he said with his right palm open as though to offer up evidence, "so the answer would likely be 'no.' You'll probably work your way up the ladder to some day become a high level operator," he did a walking gesture upwards with his left index and middle fingers as he said this, then put his hand on the table.

"You'd probably run a very clean front of a very lucrative business," he folded his arms contently.

"That stuff happens?" I asked like a baby deer. He leaned forward and glared at me.

"Where do you think all of that cash came from?" he asked as his breath hit my face.

"I get it. So it wouldn't be all that bad in the end?" I asked with another sliver of hope. "Well," Mel said leaning back, unfolding his arms, and putting his right palm out again as though he were submitting even more evidence now, "close your eyes, and open your mind to this idea. Maybe you'll meet a woman one day that loves you and whom you love?" He put his right hand down on the table.

"Yea, maybe," I said skeptically, looking away and then back into his eyes. "And maybe my brother will come back to life?" I said sarcastically.

"Don't be smart lipped with me, kid. I'm here to help you. Now shut your trap, close your eyes, open your mind, and imagine such a woman."

"Come on, Mel, I didn't hire you to be my love therapist," I said frustrated.

"Please trust me, Jack," he edged forward. "Close your eyes . . . relax . . . breathe . . . open your mind to the vast universe out there, past these walls, past your handcuffs, past that night in Venice

Beach," he said in a fatherly tone. "Open your mind to the potential inside you and to the potential out there," he pointed towards the wall next to us.

"Ok, ok," I finally submitted. I leaned back into my chair.

I closed my eyes. I envisioned a grown-up version of one of the girls with light brown or sandy blond hair who used to ride with me in the back of Frank's El Camino on the way to the beach. I imagined her name would be Grace Gordon. She had chosen a career that made her happy – perhaps a chef, magazine publisher, or photographer. I envisioned her being tall, athletic but not manly, tough but caring, pretty but able to be rough, classy and yet earthy, just like the girls I used to roll with. She also grew up to have the wisdom of Maja. I pictured Grace and me hugging one another with our eyes closed cherishing an embrace.

"I got it, Mel," I said with my eyes closed.

"Ok, good. Now," Mel said softly, "imagine you have two beautiful, healthy children with her. Picture your children with their eyes tightly closed hugging both of you."

In my mind's eye, I saw two darling children resting their heads on the sides of my leg and Grace's. The children had hair down to their shoulders. The children, like Duke and Lila, the two black Labradors in my dreams, were adorable.

"Do you have that picture firmly in your head?" Mel asked. "Yes," I said, as I nodded my head.

"Good, son. Now imagine bringing up your family while living a lie: always looking over your shoulder, covering things up, not ever showing your real life to the light of day, and, in short, living in fear."

I imagined offshore bank accounts, paying everything with cash, bodyguards at the kids' school, security systems, and a daily diet of meetings with various people in the organization about shipments, accounting, investments, and liquidations.

"Ok, I got it," I said to Mel.

"Do you think that you and Grace would be able to hold that embrace with your children without fear?"

"I don't see how we could. I'd always feel like I had to keep one eye open."

"That's right, son. And that's why you need to play ball and plead out of this thing.

You'll be able to move on with your life."

I opened my eyes:

"And that means giving testimony against Paula, Frank, and Mick?" I asked Mel.

"Yea, that is exactly what I mean," he gazed at me. "You don't have any priors. They do. The district attorney can hoist their heads up to the public as poster children of what happens when you flout the law, whereas you can ride off softly and quietly into the sunset."

"Where?"

"Witness protection," Mel said.

"Witness protection?" I asked with disbelief.

"That's what I meant when I said it was a nightmare catch 22. Even if you plead guilty to a lesser charge and get protection, you'll still be looking over your shoulder. There are the nine fellows that went down that night. They have families. And then you would have Paula, Frank, and Mick. Don't forget they have friends, too."

"But I can't testify against them. They were there to help me," I said to Mel with tears in eyes. "I love Frank. Plus, those nine bastards stabbed me."

"In that case, you would need to roll the dice and prepare yourself to live a majority of your life in . . . "

He paused to look at me. "Folsom?" I asked.

"Or somewhere like it. I'm sorry, Jack," he said with his palms out towards me as a plea. Mel stared into my eyes. "I wish I could tell you something better. Either you rat on your friends and hopefully get a lighter sentence with the understanding that you will live in fear on the outside or under witness protection, or you fight it all and risk that you will live in a place like Folsom for most of your life."

"I am so trapped," I said out loud as I looked at the ceiling in the holding cell, "and I'm not even a beaver."

CHAPTER 39

They Got You Pretty Good, Young Man

Beep, beep, beep, beep, beep, beep, beep, beep!

I awoke to the alarm clock in my Bleaker Street apartment. It was Monday morning. I was soaked with sweat. I lifted my torso off the sweat-drenched bed as quickly as I could, wiped the sweat off my eyes, and jumped off.

I jumped into the shower to make the 10:00 a.m. appointment with Mr. Rubin. I arrived around 9:45 a.m. When I got there, I rang the bell. Mr. Rubin let me inside the waiting room. I sat down on the black leather couch and started reading *New York Magazine.*

"Good morning, Jack," Arthur said with a wide smile as he exited the padded door to his private office.

"Good morning, Arthur," I said with a slight smile as I shook his extended hand. Mr. Rubin always wore a tie, but never a jacket and always had his sleeves rolled up. He was very Mr. Banana Republic. I walked with him into his office.

"You look tired, Jack," he said as he sat down on his chair. "Yea, I just had the most awful dream."

I stared at him with concern.

"Come in.Let's talk about it. Was it about making personal and not business deductions?"

He paused. "Just kidding."

I sat down on Arthur's chic looking black leather couch. He sat on his black American Leather office chair and crossed his legs.

"So tell me about this dream you had, Jack," he said as he sipped his cold water and started looking over my draft return.

I relayed the dream to him about Mel.

"Well, my cousin . . ." I used quotation marks around the word "cousin."

"Your 'cousin'?"

"Yes," I nodded. "After I called him, he picked me up from the Venice Beach party. I recall that Mick, his associate, was in the back seat. Frank's 'old lady,' or girlfriend, was driving his supped up SS car. Sitting here today, I remember Frank and Mick had UZI having submachine guns or something else on their laps. After I got in his car, Frank turned around and asked me: 'Saturn, where are they?'"

"Saturn?" Arthur asked.

"That's what Frank used to call me when I was younger. I had a Saturn car."

"Got it." Arthur said, "is that $1,000.00 purchase from Staples business or personal?" I looked at the return.

"Business – extra paper."

He nodded and made a notation.

"Did you knew where the boys were?"

"Yes. They hung out at the same place in Venice Beach every weekend."

"So what was your answer to Frank's question?"

I paused for a moment.

"I closed my eyes, like I was trying to find something I could not see, but only feel, and softly said, "I have to use the bathroom."

"What?" Frank said. "Real bad," I said.

He shrugged. So we drove to the local In N Out burger and parked. I went to the bathroom. They went to make their orders.

"Deduction – United flight to New Orleans in August?" Arthur asked. I nodded yes.

As he marked the return, he said "yeah, so what happened next?"

"As I sat there in the restroom, I thought to myself how crazy the night was. Should I go forward with the craziness and make it worse? Or stop it right there? I was shaking."

He continued to survey the return. "Did you actually use the toilet?"

"No. I just sat there. What was weird was, there was a VHS tape of *Saturday Night Live's Greatest* hits on the floor next to the toilet. I used to watch that show every Saturday night with my brother. I picked it up and glanced at it."

"It wasn't Beta?" Arthur asked. "Definitely was not Beta."

"And you had an epiphany in there?"

"Yeah, that my answer to Frank's question would be 'no.'"

"But did you second guess it?"

"Yeah. I thought this was my opportunity to get out of boring routine of life. That'd I'd regret the decision for being cowardly."

"But?"

"In a weird way, that VHS tape made me realize I had taken a wrong turn. It brought some humor in me to think of the old Gilda Radner, John Belushi, and Steve Martin skits. I mean, adapting is good, but not like this, I thought. I took a leap by coming in there, and, lo and behold, a humorous piece of the past illuminated things in the present. My second guessing receded, I flushed the toilet, and exited."

"You didn't take the tape?" He asked. I shook my head no.

"A wise decision," he looked up at me. "United flight to L.A. in September. Business?"

"Yes," I nodded.

He marked the return.

"So you get out of the restroom and what happened next?"

They were eating their burgers. Frank was on the phone. A hamburger was waiting for me.

After he got off the phone, he started kissing Paula as if nothing happened.

Mick turned to me, with a grin, and patted me on the back: "I guess we'll have to take a raincheck."

I stared at my hamburger. My hands shook as I ate it. It was the best burger I've ever tasted.

When we got back into the car, Frank said:

"'Paula, let's drop Mick off and head back to my pad. We'll patch him up there,' I remember him saying."

"What happened next?" Arthur asked.

"When we arrived at Frank's apartment, he cleaned the eight or so stab wounds with alcohol and gauze. He put new band-aids over them."

"And then?" Mr. Rubin asked.

"'Take that bed over there. The wounds should be fine in the morning,' I remember Frank saying comfortingly."

"Well, what happened in the morning?"

"In the morning, I woke up. I looked to my right and left. The whole bed was soaked with my blood. 'Frank!' I yelled out. When Frank came into the room, he said in a very calm but concerned tone: 'Saturn, we need to get you to a hospital.'"

"Maybe," Arthur said sarcastically.

"My mom came to pick me up to take me to the hospital. When I got there, they took me to the emergency room and put me on the frigid metal operating table. While I lay there, a doctor Taylor inserted several cotton Q-tips into the constellation of fresh stab wounds."

"'These things are pretty deep,' the doctor observed. I stared at him 'They got you pretty good, young man. Looks like a Wurth Phillips Head screwdriver did this – about 150 mm long in fact. You are lucky they didn't puncture your lungs with it,' I remember doctor Taylor saying."

"Was Dr. Taylor a screwdriver specialist?" Arthur asked.

I shrugged. "I figured he'd seen this type of wound before from that screwdriver." Arthur looked outside the window for a moment as if in thought. He looked back at me.

"And what did you think about when you were lying there, Jack? What ran through your head?" Arthur looked at me purposefully.

"As the Q-tips rested in the wounds, I reflected back on Liam's sudden death and the shattering of my family."

"And what did you conclude at the time?"

"That life is anarchy," I looked at Arthur. "What do you mean?"

"It is a meaningless sequence of random events."

"So you are a nihilist?" Arthur asked. "Before you answer: is this ink purchase from HP business or personal?"

"Business."

He nodded.

"What's a nihilist?" I asked out loud. "I think Nietzsche was nihilist."

"Take him – the hockey player. What do you think he believed in?" Arthur asked with a smirk.

"That life is without objective meaning, purpose, or value."

"Everything is meaningless -- so you might as well take business deductions for personal expenditures. The Nietzsche defense to an IRS audit."

I shrugged.

"So, what changed?"

"What do you mean?"

"What I mean is," at this point, Arthur leaned towards me and his tie hung down, "you are sitting in front of me, caring about the deductions you make, and so something led you to say 'I have to use the toilet' that night to Frank."

I paused to think about what he had said.

"Your actions speak louder than your words, Jack," he continued. "I guess I realized I was not Frank."

"You mean that, in that bathroom break, you had a defining moment of who you are?"

"You could say that," I put my palm out to indicate my agreement, "It is so odd. I mean, Frank was not an angel, not in any sense of the word."

"I find that hard to believe."

"But at least I knew what I was getting with Frank."

"Whereas these others looked well-bred but would take awful deductions for things like shampoo?"

"Totally. And yet my intuition told me that night that I was basically a nerd underneath.

My personal Jesus when I was growing up was the computer nerd in *WarGames*."

"The one who hacked into the government's computer system?"

"That one. But between the fifth and sixth grades I lost that nerdy chubbiness after playing basketball at the park all summer."

"That's when your brother died?"

"Yes."

"So you reinvented yourself?"

"In a way, in sixth grade, I became a jock. And yet I retained that nerdy little boy inside me who is at ease with oddballs. I guess that is why I could be around Frank, and feel comfortable with people like him, like Tubby, because . . ."

I paused and looked away from Arthur to think. He pitched in by observing:

"Because you keep an open mind. Different people have different abilities and limitations. They are not necessarily based on schooling, breeding, intelligence, how skinny they are, the clothing they wear, or even their age."

I looked at Arthur as my attention refocused back on him:

"The abilities and limitations are based on the person's experiences and character. Those items you mentioned are measurements that people . . ."

"Use to judge others," Arthur interrupted. "Exactly," I agreed.

"You know and I know that, sometimes, the measurements are right," he unlocked his legs and sat back in this chair. "Sometimes they aren't. But you can't tell, necessarily, off the bat."

I nodded.

"We've finished all of the outstanding questions I had about your return, Jack," Arthur said nicely to me with an appreciative smile. "You are doing better with your deductions," he said as he patted my back, "so please keep it up, and I'll see you next time."

CHAPTER 40

Metamorphosis: Even Worms Do It

"I'm really sorry, Jack," Arthur said to me with sympathetic eyes the next time I went to his office. He reached over and touched my knee reassuringly. "You've been audited by the IRS – you owe a few hundred thousand dollars.

I paused to gather my thoughts. I started shaking.

"Dark humor, Jack. You are actually due a credit," Arthur handed my return over. He smirked.

I reviewed the return – relieved.

"I thought about what you told me during our last meeting. It sounds like you have realized from that experience in Venice Beach that you can't," Arthur took a sip of water, "escape into any silver bullet -- whether it be routine or otherwise."

"It's like a dog trying to outrun a Ferrari," I said.

"Or even a Pinto, Jack," Mr. Rubin said warmly. "So that means you give up on life?" Mr. Rubin asked.

I adjusted myself in my seat.

"No." I looked at him with a defiant grin. "That's what I learned from the strangers who have mentored me since that night in Venice Beach."

"How so?" Arthur asked.

"Initially, after 9/11," I said. "I thought the routine of office life, where you go to the same place every day, at the same time, was isolating."

"So you concluded that routine was bad?" he asked rhetorically.

"Initially, I did. But then I learned otherwise from my friends in Italy. Seeing people you love, and who love you, on a regular basis is a great routine, like the affectionate Sicilians I met during my trip. They had dinner every week. Routines can be breath of fresh air."

"You are doing much better on your deductions. See that one there?"

"Yep."

"Good one."

As he turned to the next page in the return, I said:

"But then I tried adapting by traveling from one place to another like a vagabond, clinging to every new tree that comes along the path, so that I could forget myself."

He paused and looked up at me.

"What did you find from that?" he asked.

"That if I adapt too much away from who I am at the core, or where I need to be, I end up losing a sense of self."

"Something you were about to do that night."

I nodded.

He continued to survey the return. As he did:

"So that decision you made was all about luck then?"

"I don't think so. A WWII journalist in Chicago made it clear to me: you have to make your own luck. You won't get into the school of your dreams if you never apply."

I paused.

He turned to the next page in the return. I did, too, in mine. It was a cathartic return.

"So then what caused you to send in the application? Or even to pick up that VCR tape?"

"Well, after meeting the photographer, I kind of gathered that being lucky isn't enough. I need more. I learned from a Montana lady on a Jersey bus."

I told him about Sarah.

"That, at times, you need to take a leap of faith."

"And that is something you realize and then put into closet for safekeeping like a pair of winter socks for springtime?" Arthur asked.

He grinned.

"No," I nodded. "A woman in Brooklyn, one who lost her father on September eleventh, showed me that the only way to get out of this repeating cycle of denial, anger, and depression was to confront those demons."

"And when you say 'confront,'" Arthur said, "what do you mean?"

"Persevering. Maja and Aron, a Holocaust survivor and her husband who I met, opened my eyes to the fact that confronting those dark parts of ourselves isn't something we can do in the blink of an eye, and then call it Miller time."

"Then what is it?"

"Maja told me that perseverance requires maintenance -- like a garden." I paused.

"And that the process is not static."

"It's dynamic," Arthur said.

"Yes. I am healthy, then I may get weak, and then I fight to get healthy again."

"And yet this persistence can be a boring routine, can't it, like filing your taxes on time?"

"That is where humor comes in," I said.

"How so?" Mr. Rubin asked.

"A cancer ridden, puppeteer who resembled a pirate that I met in New Orleans had all the reason in the world to be bitter, angry, and mean."

"Yes, it certainly sounds like he did."

"But he was not. Instead, he cracked people up."

"So?" Mr. Rubin asked.

"So I learned from him that it is good to keep that sense of humor. It's like when I saw that SNL Greatest Hits tape next to the toiler in the In N Out restroom. Without a healthy sense of humor, your willingness to face uncomfortable things can fade like the sun does in the shade."

Arthur looked at me. I could tell he was reformulating his next question. And then it came:

"Today you have told me about these eight or so strangers. I wanted to ask you a question: if you could sum it up, what is the one lesson you have gleaned from meeting them?"

"There is no silver bullet, no quick fix, and no magic potion for understanding that decision so many years ago."

"The glass is *both* half full and half empty," Mr. Rubin said with a smile. "Or, with the Necker cube," he then drew a Necker cube like the one below, "which side you see in front depends on your perspective. In one view, Side A is in the front: you were a coward for not moving forward that night. In another view, Side B is in the front: you were courageous for realizing you had made a wrong turn and saying "no" to more. The cube doesn't change. It's always going to be a cube. The same goes with how you view that night, Jack."

"Precisely," I nodded.

He looked at me with appreciation, like a proud older brother or teacher. "Thoreau once said, 'Make your own Bible.'" Arthur said.

"Yeah, I respect Thoreau. He was one of founding Massachusetts transcendentalists."

"So you chose the life of an attorney that night, but little did you know it," Arthur said.

"You could say that," I said. "I guess you could say I thought to myself: if worms can do a metamorphosis into a butterfly, I can do a metamorphosis, too. And the first step to making it was taking off from Los Angeles for the unknown."

"What ever happened to that group of boys with the screwdrivers anyway?"

"Funny thing you ask. A few months after that night, there was an article in the Los Angeles Times."

"Stolen SNL Greatest Hits VHS tape found?"

"Close. The headline: CONSTRUCTION TOOL SYNDICATE: INDCITED. The article went on to explain how construction tools made by this fancy company named Wurth had been stolen – it was a massive shipment worth some millions of dollars. The article went on to mention how the syndicate was based out of Venice Beach."

"So the Wurth Phillips Head screwdriver was stolen." Arthur concluded. I shrugged – thinking back to doctor Taylor.

Arthur shuffled through some more of the return.

"Or perhaps they deducted a stolen parts purchase on their return?" He looked up with a smirk as he closed my return.

I shrugged.

At that point, our session concluded.

THE END